"Well, since now we both know where we stand, we can begin."

She looked up at him, uncertain suddenly. "Begin what?"

He flashed a smile. It had no humor in it. "Our official betrothal."

He reached down and took her hand, drawing her to her feet. His kiss was deep and sensuous, slow and possessive. His mouth moved over hers lazily...making absolutely free with her. He let her go, casually unwinding her hand from his, and letting it drop nervously to her side. Then he took her chin in his fingers and tilted it up. Her mouth was stung, lips red and swollen. Aroused.

"You are an acquisition, Andrea," he said softly, gazing down at her with gleaming possession in his eyes, "that I shall very much enjoy making."

GREEK TYCOONS

**They're the men who have everything—
except a bride...**

Wealth, power, charm—
what else could a handsome tycoon need?
In THE GREEK TYCOONS miniseries you
have already met some gorgeous Greek
multimillionaires who are in need of wives.

Now it's the turn of talented Presents author
Julia James, with her warm and sensuous romance
The Greek's Virgin Bride.

This tycoon has met his match, and he's decided
he *has* to have her...*whatever* that takes!

Prepare to meet some more Greek tycoons soon:

The Mistress Purchase
by
Penny Jordan
April 2004, #2386

The Stephanides Pregnancy
by
Lynne Graham
May 2004, #2392

Available only in Harlequin Presents®

Julia James

THE GREEK'S VIRGIN BRIDE

GREEK
TYCOONS

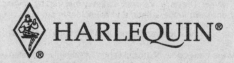

HARLEQUIN®

TORONTO • NEW YORK • LONDON
AMSTERDAM • PARIS • SYDNEY • HAMBURG
STOCKHOLM • ATHENS • TOKYO • MILAN • MADRID
PRAGUE • WARSAW • BUDAPEST • AUCKLAND

ISBN 0-373-12383-3

THE GREEK'S VIRGIN BRIDE

First North American Publication 2004.

PROLOGUE

'YOU want me to do what?' Nikos Vassilis stared at the old man seated at the desk.

Yiorgos Coustakis looked back with a level gaze. At seventy-eight he was still a formidable figure of a man. His eyes were still as piercing as they had been when he was young. They were the eyes of a man who knew the price of everything.

Especially human souls.

'You heard me.' His voice was unemotional. 'Marry my granddaughter and you can go ahead with the merger.'

'Maybe,' replied the younger man slowly. 'I just didn't believe you.'

A twisted smile pulled at Yiorgos Coustakis's mouth. 'You should,' he advised. 'It's the only deal on the table. And a deal, after all,' he said, 'is what you've flown four thousand miles for, *ne*?'

His visitor kept his hard, handsome face expressionless. Revealing anything in front of Old Man Coustakis was a major error in any kind of negotiation with him. Certainly he did not reveal the exasperation he had felt when the head of the Coustakis empire had phoned him at three a.m. in his Manhattan apartment the night before last to tell him that if he wanted a deal he'd better be in Athens this morning to sign it.

If it had been any one else phoning him Nikos would have given him short shrift. He'd had Esme Vandersee with him in bed, and sleeping was not what they'd been doing. But Yiorgos Coustakis had attractions that even the spectacular Esme, queen of the catwalk, could not compete with.

The Coustakis empire was a prize worth forgoing any woman for.

But was it a prize worth marrying a woman for? Giving up

his freedom? For a woman he'd never met? Never laid eyes on?

Nikos shifted his gaze past the penetrating dark eyes and out through the plate-glass window. Athens lay below—crowded, polluted, unique. One of the most ancient cities of Europe, the cradle of western civilisation. Nikos knew it as a child knew its parent—he had been raised on its streets, toughened in its alleyways, tempered in its unforgiving crucible.

He'd clawed his way up off the streets, fighting tooth and nail, pushing poverty behind him deal by nerve-racking deal, until now, at thirty-four, it was as if he had never been that unwanted, fatherless boy running wild in the alleyways.

The journey had been long, and tough, but he had made it— and the fruits of his triumph were sweet indeed.

Now he stood poised on the edge of his greatest triumph— getting hold of the mighty Coustakis Industries.

'I was thinking,' he said, keeping his face blank, 'of a share-swap.'

He had it all planned. He would reverse Vassilis Inc into the far larger Coustakis empire, and take the lot in a cashless exchange of shares. Oh, Old Man Coustakis would need a lot of personal financial sweeteners, he knew that, but Nikos had that covered too. He knew the old man wanted out, that his health—deny it officially as he would—was not good. But he knew Yiorgos Coustakis would never cede control of his business without a top-dollar face-saving deal—he'd go out like a lion, with a final roar, not like an old wolf driven from the pack.

That didn't bother Nikos—when his time came to quit he'd drive a hard bargain too, just to keep his successor on his toes.

But what Coustakis had just thrown at him had winded him like a blow to the gut. Marry his granddaughter to get hold of the company? Nikos hadn't even known the old man *had* a granddaughter!

Inside, behind the mask that was the carefully schooled expression on his face, Nikos had to tip his hat to the old man.

He could still catch his rivals out—even a rival who was posing as a friendly merger partner.

'You can have the share-swap—on your wedding day.'

Yiorgos's reply was flat. Nikos kept his silence. Behind his composed appearance his mind was teeming. Racing.

'Well?' Yiorgos prompted him.

'I'll think about it,' returned Nikos. His voice was cool.

He turned to go.

'Walk out the door and the deal is off. Permanently.'

Nikos stopped. He rested his eyes on the man seated at the desk. He wasn't bluffing. Nikos knew that. Everyone knew Old Man Coustakis never bluffed.

'You sign now, or not at all.'

Nikos's slate-grey eyes—a legacy from his unknown father, as was his un-Greek height of well over six feet—met with Coustakis's black ones. For a long, timeless moment, they held. Then slowly, unflinchingly, Nikos Vassilis walked back to the desk, picked up the gold pen Yiorgos Coustakis silently handed him, and signed the document lying there.

Without a word, he set down the pen and walked out.

On his brief journey down to ground level in the plush executive lift in the Coustakis HQ, Nikos tried in vain to rein in his thoughts.

Exultation ran side by side with anger—exultation that his longed-for goal was now within his grasp, anger that he had been outmanoeuvred by the wiliest fox he knew.

He straightened his shoulders. Who cared if Coustakis had driven a bargain he hadn't even seen coming? No one could have. The man played his cards closer to his chest than anyone Nikos knew—himself included. And if he could suddenly produce a granddaughter out of thin air that no one had ever heard of till now, well, what did it matter to him, Nikos Vassilis, who was going to get what he'd wanted all his life—a safe, secure, glittering place at the very top of the greasy pole he'd been climbing all his life?

That the unknown granddaughter fated to be his wife was a

complete stranger was an irrelevance compared with taking over the Coustakis empire.

He knew what mattered in his life. What had always mattered.

And Old Man Coustakis—and his granddaughter—held the key to his dreams.

Nikos was not about to turn it down.

CHAPTER ONE

ANDREA could hear her mother coughing wheezily in the kitchen as she made breakfast. Her face tensed. It was getting worse, that cough. Kim had been asthmatic all her life, Andrea knew, but for the last eighteen months the bronchitis she'd got the winter before had never been shaken off, and her lungs were weaker than ever.

The doctor had been sympathetic but, apart from keeping Kim on her medication, all he'd advised was spending the winter in a warmer, drier climate. Andrea had smiled with grim politeness, and not bothered to tell him that he might as well have said she should take her mother to the moon. They barely had enough to cover their living expenses as it was, let alone to go gallivanting off abroad.

A clunk through the letterbox of the council flat she'd lived in all her life told Andrea that the post had arrived. She hurried off to get it before her mother could get to the door. The post only brought bills, and every bill brought more worries. Already her mother was fretting about how they would be able to pay for heating in the coming winter.

Andrea glanced at the post as she scooped it off the worn carpet by the front door. Two bills, some junk mail, and a thick cream-coloured envelope with her name typed on it. She frowned. Now what? An eviction order? A debt reminder? Something unpleasant from the council? Or the bank?

She ripped her thumbnail down the back and yanked open the paper inside, unfolding it. She caught a glimpse of some ornate heading, and a neatly typed paragraph—'Dear Ms Fraser....'

As she read, Andrea's body slowly froze. Twice she re-read the brief missive. Then, with a contortion of blind rage on her

9

face, she screwed the letter into a ball and hurled it with all her force at the door. It bounced, and lay on the carpet.

Andrea had heard the phrase 'red-misting'—now she knew first-hand what it meant.

Bastard!

She felt her hands fist in anger at her side. Then, with a deep, controlling breath, she made herself open her palms, bend down, and pick up the letter. She must not let Kim find it.

All that day the contents of the letter, jammed into the bottom of her bag, burned at her, the terse paragraph it contained repeating itself over and over again in Andrea's head.

> *You are required to attend Mr Coustakis at the end of next week. Your airline ticket will be at Heathrow for you to collect on Friday morning. Consult the enclosed itinerary for your check-in time. You will be met at Athens airport. You should phone the number below to acknowledge receipt of this communication by five p.m. tomorrow.*

It was simply signed 'For Mr Coustakis'.

Dark emotions flowed through Andrea. 'Mr Coustakis's.' Aka Yiorgos Coustakis. Founder and owner of Coustakis Industries, worth hundreds of millions of pounds. A man Andrea loathed with every atom of her being.

Her grandfather.

Not that Yiorgos Coustakis had ever acknowledged the relationship. Memory of another letter leapt in Andrea's mind. That one had been written directly to her mother. It had been brief, too, and to the point. It had informed Kim Fraser, in a single, damning sentence, that any further attempt to communicate with Mr Coustakis would result in legal action being taken against her. That had been ten years ago. Yiorgos Coustakis had made it damningly clear that his granddaughter simply didn't exist as far as he was concerned.

Now, out of the blue, she had been summoned to his presence.

Andrea's mouth tightened. Did he really think she would meekly pack her bags and check in for a flight to Athens next Friday? Darkness shadowed her eyes. Yiorgos Coustakis could drop dead before she showed up!

A second letter arrived the next day, again from the London office of Coustakis Industries. Its contents were even terser.

Dear Ms Fraser,
You failed to communicate your receipt of the letter dated two days ago. Please do so immediately.

Like the first letter, Andrea took it into work—Kim must definitely not see it. She had suffered far too much from the father of the man she had loved so desperately—so briefly. A sick feeling sloshed in Andrea's stomach. How could anyone have treated her gentle, sensitive mother so brutally? But Yiorgos Coustakis had—and had relished it.

Andrea typed a suitable reply, keeping it as barely civil as the letters she had received. She owed nothing to the sender. Not even civility. Nothing but hatred.

With reference to your recent correspondence, you should note that any further letters to me will continue to be ignored.

She printed it out and signed it with her bare name—hard and uncompromising.

Like the stock she came from.

Nikos Vassilis swirled the fine vintage wine consideringly in his glass.

'So, when will my bride arrive, Yiorgos?' he enquired of his host.

He was dining with his grandfather-in-law-to-be in the vast, over-decorated house on the outskirts of Athens that Yiorgos Coustakis considered suitable to his wealth and position.

'At the end of the week,' his host answered tersely.

He didn't look well, Nikos noted. His colour was high, and there was a pinched look around his mouth.

'And the wedding?'

His host gave a harsh laugh. 'So eager? You don't even know what she looks like!'

Nikos's mobile mouth curled cynically.

'Her looks, or lack of them, are not going to be a deal-breaker, Yiorgos,' he observed sardonically.

Yiorgos gave another laugh. Less harsh this time. Coarser.

'Bed her in the dark, if you must! I had to do that with her grandmother!'

A sliver of distaste filtered through Nikos. Though no one would dare say it to his face, the world knew that Yiorgos Coustakis had won his richly dowered, well-born wife by dint of getting the poor girl so besotted with him that she'd agreed to meet him in his apartment one afternoon. Yiorgos, as ambitious as he was ruthless, had made sure the information leaked to Marina's father, who had arrived in time to prevent Yiorgos having to undergo the ordeal of sex with a plain, drab dab of a girl in daylight, but not in time to save her reputation. 'Who will believe she left my apartment a virgin?' Yiorgos had challenged her father callously—and won his bride.

Nikos flicked his mind back to the present. Was he insane, going through with this? Marrying a woman he hadn't set eyes on just because she happened to have a quarter of Yiorgos Coustakis's DNA? Idly he found himself wondering if the girl felt the same way about marrying a complete stranger. Then he shrugged mentally—in the world of the very rich, dynastic marriages were commonplace. The Coustakis girl would have been reared from birth to know that she was destined to be a pawn in her grandfather's machinations. She would be pampered and doll-like, her primary skill that of spending money in huge amounts on clothes, jewellery and anything else she took a fancy to.

Well, Nick acknowledged silently, glancing around the opulent dining room, she would certainly have money to spare as his wife! Once he'd taken over Coustakis Industries his income would be ten times what it already was—she could squander it on anything she wanted! Spending money would keep her busy, and keep her happy.

He paused momentarily. With a wife in the background he would obviously have to keep his personal life more low-profile. He would not be one of those husbands, all too familiar in the circles he now moved in, who thought nothing of flaunting their mistresses in front of their families. Nevertheless, he had no intention of altering the very enjoyable private life he indulged himself in, even if he would have to be more discreet about it once he was married.

Oh, he was well aware that as a rich man he could have been as old as Methuselah and as ugly as sin and beautiful women would still have fawned on him. Wealth was the most powerful aphrodisiac to those kind of women. Of course even when he'd been dirt-poor women had always come easily to him—another legacy from his philandering father, no doubt. One of Esme's many predecessors had said to his face, as she lay exhausted and sated beneath him, that if he ever ran out of money he could make a fortune hiring himself out as a stud. Nikos had laughed, his mouth widening wolfishly, and turned her over...

He shifted in his uncomfortably ornate chair. Thinking about sex was not a good idea right now. His razor-sharp mind might not have objected to kow-towing to Old Man Coustakis's summons that night, but his body was reminding him that it had been deprived of its customary satiation. Even though he'd put in extra time these last few days at the gym and on the squash courts in the exclusive health club he belonged to, Nikos could feel a familiar tightening that presaged sexual desire.

As soon as he decently could he'd take his leave tonight and phone Xanthe Palloupis. She was an extremely complaisant mistress—always welcoming, always responsive to his physical needs. Even though it had been three months since he'd last visited her—Esme Vandersee had replaced her over two months ago—he knew she would greet him warmly at her discreetly located but very expensive apartment, confident that he would tell her in the morning she could go to her favourite jeweller's and order something to remember his visit by.

Would he keep her on when he had married this unknown granddaughter of Yiorgos Coustakis? She had other lovers, he knew, and it did not trouble him. Esme, too, right this moment was doubtless consoling her wounded—and highly developed!—ego by letting another of her crowded court do the honours by her. As a top model she always had men slavering after her, but for all that Nikos knew perfectly well that he would only have to snap his fingers and she would come instantly to his heel—and other parts of his anatomy.

He shifted uncomfortably in his seat again. He definitely needed some energetic physical release before his wedding night! The Coustakis girl would be a virgin, of course, and bedding her would be more of a duty, not a pleasure, though he would be as careful with her as was possible. He'd never taken a virgin—he would have to make totally sure he was not sexually frustrated on his wedding night or she'd be the one to suffer from it, however plain she was.

Just how plain was she? Nikos wondered, his mind running on. He had a pretty shrewd idea that from the tinge of open malice in Yiorgos's expression when he'd made that coarse comment about bedding her in the dark she had no looks at all. The old man probably thought it amusing that a man who was never seen without a beautiful woman hanging on his arm should now be hog-tied to a female whose sole attraction was as the gateway to control and eventual ownership of Coustakis Industries.

Another thought flitted through his mind. Just who exactly was this unknown granddaughter of Yiorgos Coustakis? One of the main attractions of taking over Coustakis Industries was that Yiorgos had no offspring to fight him for control. His only son had been killed in a smash-up years ago. Marina Coustakis had had some kind of seizure, so the gossip went, and had become a permanent invalid—though not managing to die until a few years ago. That meant that Yiorgos had not been free to marry again and beget more heirs. But then, mused Nikos, if the son had indeed been married when he died, and the grand-daughter already born, maybe that hadn't mattered too much to Yiorgos. The son's widow had presumably married again and was out of the picture, apart from having dutifully reared the Coustakis granddaughter to be a docile, well-behaved, well-bred Greek wife.

Her docility would certainly make things easier for him, Nikos thought. Oh, he wouldn't flaunt his sex-life in her face, but obviously her mother would have taught her that husbands strayed, that it was in their nature, and that her role was to be a dutiful spouse, immaculate social hostess and attentive mother.

Nikos's hand stilled a moment as he raised his wine glass to his mouth. Yiorgos was retelling the drama of some coup he'd pulled off years ago, clearly relishing the memory of having beaten off a rival, bankrupting him in the process, and Nikos was only paying attention with a quarter of his mind. Three-quarters of it was considering what it would be like to be a father.

Because that, he knew, was what all this was about. Yiorgos was approaching the end of his life—he wanted to know his DNA would continue. He wanted an heir.

And Nikos? Strange feelings pricked at him. What did he know about fatherhood? His own father didn't even know he existed—he'd impregnated his mother and sailed with the tide at dawn. He could even be alive somewhere, Nikos knew. It meant nothing to him. His mother had scarcely mentioned him—she'd worked in a bar, when she'd worked at all, and her maternal instincts had not been well developed. Her son's existence hadn't been important to her, and when he'd left home as a teenager she'd hardly noticed. As he had slowly, painfully, begun to make money, she'd accepted his hand-outs without question, let alone interest, and hadn't lived to see him make real money. She'd been knocked down by a taxi twelve years ago, when he was twenty-two. Nikos had given her an expensive funeral.

He lifted the wine glass to his mouth and drank. It was a

rare, costly vintage, he knew—learning about wines and all the other fine things of life was information he'd gathered along the way. He relished all fine things, and once he ran Coustakis Industries the finest things in the world would be his for the taking. He would have taken his place not just amongst the wealthy, as he now was, but amongst the super-rich. And if Coustakis wanted him to impregnate his granddaughter and give him a great-grandson—well, he could do that.

Whatever she looked like.

Andrea stood by the front door of the flat, staring at the opened letter. It was not from Coustakis Industries. It was from one of London's most prestigious department stores, and informed her that enclosed was a gold store card with an immediate credit limit of five thousand pounds. It further stated her that all invoices incurred by her to that limit would be forwarded to the private office of Yiorgos Coustakis for payment. A second opened letter underlaid the one from the store. That one *was* from Coustakis Industries, and it instructed her to make use of the store card that would be sent under separate cover in order to provide herself with a suitable wardrobe for when she attended Mr Coustakis at the end of the following week. It finished with a reminder to phone the London office to confirm receipt of these instructions.

Andrea's dark eyes narrowed dangerously. What the hell was the old bastard playing at?

What did he want? What was going on? Her scalp prickled with unease. She didn't like this—she didn't like it at all!

Her brain was in turmoil. What would happen if she did what she wanted to do and cut the store card in half and sent it back to her grandfather with orders to stick it where it hurt? Would he get the message? Somehow she didn't think so.

Yiorgos Coustakis wanted something from her. He'd never acknowledged her existence before. But he was a rich man—very rich. And rich men had power. And they used it to get their own way.

Her face set. What could Yiorgos Coustakis do to them if

he wanted to? Kim had debts—Andrea hated to think of them, let alone the reason for those debts, but they were there, like a millstone round their necks. Both of them, mother and daughter, worked endlessly, repaying them little by little, and given another five years or so they finally would be clear. But that was a long way off.

And Kim's health was getting worse.

Anguish crushed Andrea's heart like a vice. Her mother had suffered so *much*—she'd had such a rotten life. A brief, tiny glimpse of happiness when she was twenty, a few golden weeks in her youth, and then it had been destroyed. Totally destroyed. And she'd spent the next twenty-four years of her life being the most devoted, caring, *loving* mother than anyone could ask for.

I just wish we could get out, Andrea thought for the millionth time. The high-rise block they lived in was overdue for repairs, though she could understand the council's reluctance to spend good money on doing up an estate when half its population would simply start to trash it the moment the paint was dry. The flats themselves had a list as long as your arm of repairs needed—the worst was that the damp in the kitchen and bathroom was dire, which did no good at all for Kim's asthma. The lift was usually broken, and anyway usually served as a late-night public convenience, not to mention a place for scoring drugs.

For a brief, fleeting second Andrea thought of the immense wealth of Yiorgos Coustakis.

Then put it behind her.

She would have nothing to do with such a man. *Nothing.*

Whatever he planned for her.

CHAPTER TWO

NIKOS pushed the sleeve of his suit jacket back and glanced at the slim gold watch circling his lean wrist. What had Old Man Coustakis called him here for? He'd been cooling his heels on the shaded terrace for over ten minutes—and ten minutes was a long time for a man as busy as Nikos Vassilis. He did not like waiting patiently—he was a man in a hurry. Always had been.

The manservant approached again, from the large double doors leading into the opulent drawing room beyond, and deferentially asked him if he would like another drink. Curtly, Nikos shook his head, and asked—again—when Mr Coustakis would be ready to see him. The manservant replied that he would enquire, and padded off silently.

Irritated, Nikos turned and stared out over the gardens spread below. They were highly ornate, clearly designed to impress, not to provide a pleasant place to stroll around. Nikos had a sudden vision of a small boy trying to play out there and finding nothing but expensive specimen plants, and fussy paths and over-planted borders. His mouth tightened unconsciously. If he were to become a father he would need a decent place to raise his family…

His mind sheered away. The reality of what he was about to do—marry Yiorgos Coustakis's plain, pampered granddaughter, a female he'd never met—was starting to hit him. Could he really go through with it? Even to get hold of Coustakis Industries?

He shook the doubts from his mind. Of course he would go through with it! Anyway, it wasn't as if he were signing his life away. Old Man Coustakis would not live for ever. In half a dozen years he would probably be dead, and then Nikos and the unknown granddaughter could come to some sort of civilised divorce, go their separate ways, and that would be that.

And what about your son? What will he think about your 'civilised divorce'?

He pushed that thought from his mind as well. Who knew? Maybe the granddaughter would turn out to be barren, as well as plain as sin.

A footfall behind him made him turn.

And freeze.

Nikos's eyes narrowed as he saw the unfamiliar woman step onto the wide sweeping terrace where he stood. The cloud of dark bronze hair rustled on her shoulders, making him take notice of her long, slender neck. Then, as if a brief glance were tribute enough for that particular feature, his eyes clamped back to her face.

Theos, but she was a stunner! Her skin was paler than a Greek's, but still tanned. She had a short, delicate nose, sculpted cheeks, and a wide, generous mouth. Her eyes were like rich chestnut, the lashes ridiculously long and smoky.

He felt his body kick with pleasure at looking at her. As of their own volition, his eyes wandered downwards again, past that slender neck framed by that glorious hair, down over full, swelling breasts, superbly moulded by the tight-fitting jacket she wore, nipping in to a deliciously spannable waist, and then ripening outwards to softly rounded hips, before descending down long, long legs.

He frowned. She was wearing trousers. The sight offended him. With legs that long she should be wearing a short, tight skirt that hugged those splendid thighs and clung lovingly to the lush, rounded bottom he felt sure a woman like that must have...

Who the hell was she?

His brain interrupted his body's visceral contemplation of the female's physical attributes. What was a woman this lush, this drop-dead gorgeous, this damn *sexy*, doing here in Yiorgos Coustakis's house?

The answer came like a blow to the gut. There was only one

reason a woman who looked like this would be swanning around Old Man Coustakis's private residence, and that was because she was a private guest. Very private.

All of Athens knew that Yiorgos Coustakis liked to keep a stable of women. He was renowned for it, even from long before his wife became an invalid.

And they'd always been young women—even as he'd got older.

Even now, apparently.

Distaste filled Nikos's mouth. OK, so maybe the old man was still up for it, even at his age, but the idea of the man of seventy-eight keeping a woman who couldn't be more than twenty-five, if that, as his mistress was repugnant in the extreme.

Andrea blinked, momentarily blinded by the bright light after the dim shade of the interior of the huge house she had been deposited at barely five minutes ago by the lush limo that had met her at the airport.

Then, as her vision cleared, she saw someone was already on the terrace. She took in an impression of height, and darkness. Black hair, a sleek, powerful-looking business suit, an immaculately knotted tie—and a face that made her stop dead.

The skin tone was Mediterranean; there was no doubt about that. But what struck her incongruously was the pair of piercing steel-grey eyes that blazed at her. She felt her stomach lurch, and blinked again. She went on staring, taking in, once she could drag her eyes away from those penetrating grey ones, a strong, straight nose, high cheekbones and a wide, firm mouth.

She shook her head slightly, as if to make sure the man she was staring at was really there.

Suddenly Andrea saw the man's expression change. Harden with disapproval. And something more than disapproval. Disdain. Something flared inside her—and it was nothing to do with the unmistakable frisson that had sizzled through her like a jolt of electricity in the face of the blatant appraisal this startlingly breath-catching man had just subjected her to. She would have been blind not to have registered the look of out-right sexual attraction in the man's face when he'd first set eyes on her a handful of seconds ago. She was used to that reaction in men. For the most part it was annoying more than anything, and over the years she had learnt to dress down, concealing the ripeness of her figure beneath loose, baggy clothes, confining her glowing hair into a subdued plait, and seldom bothering with make-up. Besides—a familiar shaft of bitterness stabbed at her—she knew all too well that any initial sexual attraction men showed in her would not last—not when they saw the rest of her...

She pulled her mind away, washing out bitterness with an even more familiar upsurge of raw, desperate gratitude—to her mother, to fate, to any providential power, to everyone who had helped her along her faltering way in the long, painful years until she had emerged to take her place as a functioning adult in the world. Considering what the alternatives might have been, she had no cause for bitterness—none at all.

And if she felt bitter about the man who was her father's father—well, that was not on her own behalf, only her mother's. For her mother's sake *only* she was here, now, standing on this terrace, over a thousand miles from home—being looked at disdainfully by a man she could not drag her eyes from.

It had been a hard decision to make. It had been her friends Tony and Linda who had helped her make it.

'But why is he *doing* this?' she'd asked them, for the dozenth time. 'He's up to something and I don't know what—and that worries me!'

'Maybe he just wants to get to know you, Andy,' said Linda peaceably. 'Maybe he's old, and ill, and wants to make up for how he treated you.'

'Oh, so that's why I've been getting letters just about ordering me to go and dance attendance on him! *And* not a dickey-bird about Mum, either! No, if he'd really wanted to make up he'd have written more politely—and to Mum, not me.'

'If you want my advice I think you should go out there,' said Linda's husband, Tony. 'Like Linda said, he *might* be after a reconciliation, but even if he isn't, suppose he wants to use you for his own nefarious ends in some way? That, you know, puts you in a strong position. Have you thought of that?'

Andrea frowned.

Tony went on. 'Look, if he does want you for something, then if he doesn't want you to refuse he's going to have to do something *you* want.'

'Like what?' Andrea snorted. 'He doesn't have a thing I want!'

'He's got money, Andy,' Tony said quietly. 'Shed-loads of it.'

Andrea's eyes narrowed to angry slits. 'He can choke on it for all I care! I don't want a penny from him!'

'But what about your mum, Andy?' said Tony, even more quietly.

Andrea stilled. Tony pressed on, leaning forward. 'What if he forked out enough for her to clear her debts—and move to Spain?'

Andrea's breath seemed tight in her chest. As tight as her mother's breath was, day in, day out. Instantly in her mind she heard her mother's dry, asthmatic cough, saw her pause by the sink, breathing slowly and painfully, her frail body hunched.

'I can't,' she answered faintly. 'I can't take that man's money!'

'Think it through,' urged Tony. 'You wouldn't be taking his money for yourself, but for your mum. He owes her—you've always said that and it's true! She's raised you single-handed with nothing from him except insults and abuse! He lives in the lap of luxury, worth hundreds of millions, and his grand-daughter lives in a council flat. Do it for her, Andy.'

And that, in the end, had been the decider. Though every fibre of her being wanted never, ever to have anything to do with the man who had treated her mother so callously, the moment Tony had said 'Spain' a vista had opened up in Andrea's mind so wonderful she knew she could not refuse. If she could just get her grandfather to buy her mother a small apartment somewhere it was warm and dry all year round...

It was for that very reason that Andrea was now standing on the terrace of her grandfather's palatial property in Athens.

She would get her mother the dues owed her.

She gave a smile as she looked again at the impressive man who stood before her. A small, tight, defiant—dismissive—smile. So, he knew who she was, did he, Mr Mega-Cool? He looked so sleek, screaming 'money' in his superbly tailored suit, with his immaculately cut dark hair, the gleam of gold at his wrist as he paused in the action of checking his watch—oh, he must be one of her grandfather's entourage. No doubt. One of his business associates, partners—whatever rich men called each other in their gilded world where the price of electricity was an irrelevance and there was never green mould on the bathroom walls...

So much, she thought with self-mocking acknowledgement, for the shopping spree she'd been on with Linda and Tony in that ultra posh London department store, courtesy of its gold store card! She'd thought the outrageously priced trouser suit she'd bought, shouting its designer label, would do the trick—fool anyone who saw her that the last thing she could possibly be was a common-as-muck London girl off a housing estate! And Linda had even done her hair and make-up that morning, before she'd set out for the airport, making her look svelte and expensive to go with the fantastic new outfit she'd travelled in. Obviously she need not have bothered!

The man looking at her so disdainfully out of those cold steel-grey eyes knew perfectly well what she was—who she was. Yiorgos Coustakis's cheap-and-nasty bastard granddaughter!

Her chin went up. Well, what did she care? She had her own opinions of Yiorgos Coustakis—and they were not generous. So if this man standing here on her grandfather's mile-long terrace, looking down his strong, straight nose at her, his mouth tight with disdain, thought she wasn't fit for a palatial place like this, what was it to her? Zilch. Just as Yiorgos Coustakis was nothing to her—nothing except the price of some small, modest reparation to the woman he had treated like dirt...

Her eyes hardened. Nikos saw their expression change, saw the derisive smile, the insolent tilt of the woman's chin. Clearly the female was shameless about her trade! The distaste he felt about Old Man Coustakis keeping a mistress at his age filtered into distaste for the woman herself. It checked the stirring of his own body, busy responding the way nature liked it to do when in the presence of a sexually alluring female.

So when the woman strolled towards him, the smile on her face unable to compensate for the hardness in her eyes, he responded in kind.

Andrea saw the withdrawal in his eyes, and suddenly, like a cloud passing in front of the sun, she felt a chill emanate from him. Suddenly he wasn't just a breath-catchingly, heart-stoppingly handsome man, looking a million dollars, tall and lean—he was an icily formidable, hard-eyed, patrician-born captain of industry who looked on the rest of humanity as his inferior minions...

Well, tough! She tilted her head, almost coquettishly, letting her glorious hair riot over her shoulders. An intense desire to annoy him came over her.

'Hi,' she breathed huskily. 'We haven't met, have we? I'd remember, I know!' She let a gleam of appreciation enter her glowing eyes. That would annoy him even more; she instinctively knew.

She held her hand out. It was looking beautiful—Linda had given her a manicure the night before, smoothing the work-roughened skin and putting on nail extensions and a rich nail-varnish whose colour matched her hair.

Nikos ignored the hand. A revulsion against touching flesh that had caressed, for money, a rich old man, filled him. It didn't matter that half his body was registering renewed arousal at the sound of that breathy voice, the heady fragrance of her body as she approached him. He subdued it ruthlessly.

Besides, it had just registered with him that the woman was English. That would account for the auburn colouring.

Presumably, he found himself thinking, for a woman of her profession hair that colour would command a premium in lands where dark hair was the norm.

The man's rejection of her outstretched hand made Andrea falter. She let her hand fall to her side. But still, despite the shut-out, she refused to be intimidated. After all, if she failed at the first test—being sneered at by a complete stranger for being the bastard Coustakis granddaughter—then she would be doomed to fail in her mission. Intimidation was, she knew from the painfully extracted reminiscences of her mother's abrupt expulsion from Greece twenty-four years ago, the forte of the man who had summoned her here like a servant. She must not, above all, be intimidated by Yiorgos Coustakis as her mother had been. She must stand up to him—give him as good as she got. Tony's words echoed in her mind—if he had summoned her here, he wanted something. And that made her position powerful.

She had to remember that. *Must* remember that.

She was in enemy territory. Confidence was everything.

So now, in the face of the obvious disdain of this stunning stranger, she refused to be cowed. Instead, she gave that derisive little smile again, deliberately tossed her head and, shooting him a mocking glance, strolled right past him to take in the view over the grounds. She leant her palms on the stone balustrade, taking some of the weight off her legs. They were aching slightly, probably tension more than anything, because she'd been sitting down most of the day—first in the luxurious airline seat and then in the luxurious chauffeur-driven car. Still, she must do her exercises tonight—right after she'd phoned Tony, as they'd arranged.

Her mind raced, thinking about all the safety nets that she and Tony had planned out. The man behind her was totally forgotten. However good-looking he was—however scornful of the Coustakis bastard granddaughter—he was not important. What was important was going through, for the thousandth time, everything she and Tony had done to make sure that her grandfather could not outmanoeuvre her. Had they left any holes? Left anything uncovered?

Working on the premise that Yiorgos Coustakis was totally ruthless in getting what he wanted, she and Tony had planned elaborate measures to make sure that Andrea always had an escape route if she needed one. The first was to ensure that every evening of her stay in Greece she would phone Tony on the mobile he had lent her. If he did not hear from her by eleven p.m., he was to alert the British consul in Athens and tell them a British citizen was being forcibly held against her will. And if that did not do the trick—her mouth tightened— then Tony's second phone call would be to a popular British tabloid, spilling the whole story of how the granddaughter of one of the richest men in Europe came to be living on a council estate. Yiorgos Coustakis might be immune to bad publicity, but she wondered whether his shareholders would be as sanguine about the stink she could raise if she wanted…

And then, if her grandfather still didn't want to let her go, she had left her passport, together with seven hundred euros, plus her return ticket, in a secure locker at Athens airport—the key to which was in her make-up bag. She had also, not trusting her grandfather an inch, purchased a second, open-dated ticket to London while she was still at Heathrow, which she had not yet collected from the airline. She had paid for that one herself.

Andrea smiled grimly as she stared out over the ornate, fussily designed gardens. Though she hadn't been able to afford to buy the full-price ticket from her own meagre funds, she had come up with a brilliant idea for how to pay for it. The day that she and Tony and Linda had gone into the West End to buy her outfit, they had also visited the store's jewellery department. The balance from the five thousand pounds after buying the trouser suit and accessories had purchased a very nice pearl necklace—so nice that they had immediately taken it to another jewellery shop and sold it for cash. With the money they had bought the airline ticket, a wad of traveller's cheques, and split the rest into a combination of sterling, US dollars and euros. That, surely, she thought, her eyes quite unseeing of the view in front of her, should be enough to ensure that she could simply leave whenever she wanted.

Behind her, Nikos Vassilis had stiffened. The woman had simply walked past him as if he were no one! And that derisive little smile and mocking look of hers sent a shaft of anger through him! No woman did that to him! Certainly not one who stooped to earn her living in such a way. He stared after her, eyes narrowing.

Then a discreet cough a little way to his side caught his attention, as it was designed to do. The manservant was back, murmuring politely that Mr Coustakis would see him now, if he would care to come this way.

With a last, ireful glance at the woman now leaning carelessly on the balustrade, totally ignoring him, her hair a glorious sunset cloud around her shoulders, Nikos stalked off into the house.

CHAPTER THREE

AN HOUR later, as she was shown into the dim, shaded room, Andrea straightened her shoulders, ready for battle. At first it seemed the room was empty. Then a voice startled her.

'Come here.'

The voice was harsh, speaking in English. Clearly issuing an order.

She walked forward. She seemed to be in a sort of library, judging from the shelves of books layering every wall. Her heels sounded loud on the parquet flooring. She could see, now, that a large desk was positioned at the far end of the room, and behind it a man was sitting.

It seemed to take a long time to reach him. One part of her brain realised why—it was a deliberate ploy to put anyone entering the room at a disadvantage to the man already sitting at the desk.

As she walked forward she glanced around her, quite deliberately letting her head crane around, taking in her surroundings, as if the man at the desk were of no interest to her. Her heels clicked loudly.

She reached the front of the desk, and only then did she deign to look at the man who had summoned her.

It was the eyes she noticed first. They were deepset, in sunken sockets. His whole face was craggy and wrinkled, very old, but the eyes were alight. They were dark, almost black in this dim light, but they scoured her face.

'So,' said Yiorgos Coustakis to his granddaughter, whom he had never set eyes on till now, 'you are that slut's brat.' He nodded. 'Well, no matter. You'll do. You'll have to.'

His eyes went on scouring her face. Inside, as the frail bud of hope that maybe Yiorgos Coustakis had softened his hard heart died a swift, instant death, Andrea fought to quell the upsurge of blind rage as she heard him refer to her mother in such a way. With a struggle, she won the battle. Losing her temper and storming out now would get her nowhere except back to London empty-handed. Instead, she opted for silence.

She went on standing there, being inspected from head to toe.

'Turn around.'

The order was harsh. She obeyed it.

'You walk perfectly well.'

The brief sentence was an accusation. Andrea said nothing.

'Have you a tongue in your head?' Yiorgos Coustakis demanded.

She went on looking at him.

Was a man's soul in his eyes, as the proverb said? she wondered. If so, then Yiorgos Coustakis's soul was in dire condition. The black eyes that rested on her were the most terrifying she had ever seen. They seemed to bore right into her —and, search as she would, she could see nothing in them to reassure her. Not a glimmer of kindness, of affection, even of humour, showed in them. A feeling of profound sadness filled her, and she realised that, despite all the evidence, something inside her had been hoping against hope that the man she had grown up hating and despising was not such a man after all.

But he was proving exactly the callous monster she had always thought him.

'Why did you bring me here?'

The question fell from her lips without her thinking. But instinctively she knew she had done the right thing in taking the battle—for this was a battle, no doubt about that now, none at all—to her grandfather.

He saw it, and the dark eyes darkened even more.

'Do not speak to me in that tone,' he snapped, throwing his head back.

Her chin lifted in response.

'I have come over a thousand miles at your bidding. I am entitled to know why.' Her voice was as steady as she could make it, though in her breast she could feel her heart beating wildly.

His laugh came harsh, scornful.

'You are entitled to nothing! *Nothing!* Oh, I know why you came! The moment you caught a glimpse of the kind of money you could spend if you came here you changed your tune! Why do you think I sent you that store card? I knew that would flush you out!' He leant forward, his once-powerful arms leaning on the surface of the polished mahogany desk. 'But understand this, and understand it well! You will be on the first plane back to London unless you do exactly, *exactly* what I want you to do! Understand me?'

His eyes flashed at her. She held his gaze, though it was like a heavy weight on her. So, she thought, Tony had been right—he *did* want something from her. But what? She needed to know. Only when she knew what the man sitting there, who by a vile accident of fate just happened to be her grandfather, wanted of her could she start to bargain for the money she wanted from him.

Play it cool, girl…play it cool…

She lifted an interrogative eyebrow.

'And what is it, *exactly*, that you want me to do?'

His brows snapped together at the sarcastic emphasis she gave to echo his.

'You'll find out—when I want you to.' He held up a hand, silencing her. 'I've had enough of you for now. You will go to your room and prepare yourself for dinner. We will have a guest. With your upbringing you obviously won't know how to comport yourself, so I shall tell you now that you had better change your attitude! In *this* country a woman knows how to behave—see that you do not shame me in my own house! Now, go!'

Andrea turned and left. The walk back to the door seemed much further than it had in the opposite direction. Her heart was pounding.

It went on pounding all the way back upstairs to her room. She shut the door and leant against it. So, that was her grandfather! That was the man whose son had had a brief, whirlwind romance with her mother, who had thrown her, pregnant and penniless, out of the country, and left her to bear and raise his grandchild in poverty, refusing to acknowledge her existence.

She owed such a man nothing. Nothing! Not duty, nor respect—and certainly not loyalty or affection.

What does he want of me?

The question went round and round, unanswered. Fretting at her.

In the end, to calm herself down and pass the time, she decided to make use of the opulent bathroom. Inside its lavish, overdone interior she could not but help revel in the luxury it offered.

The bath was vast, and it had, she discovered, sinking into its deep scented depths, whirling jets that massaged her body, easing the aching muscles in her tense legs. Blissfully, she gave herself to the wonderful sensation. Towering bubbles from the half a bottle of bath foam she'd emptied in veiled her whole body, from breasts to feet.

You walk perfectly well...

She heard the harsh accusation ring in her head again, and her mouth tightened.

When she emerged from the bathroom, entering her lavishly decorated bedroom suite, swathed in a floor-length towel, it was to see a maid at the open door of her closet, hanging up clothes. The girl turned, bobbing a brief curtsey, and hesitantly informed Andrea that she was here to help her dress.

'I don't need any help,' said Andrea tersely.

The girl looked subdued, and Andrea immediately regretted her tone of voice.

'Please,' she said temporisingly, 'it's quite unnecessary.'

She walked past the huge bed, covered in a heavy gold and white patterned bedspread, and across to the room-sized closet. Whatever Yiorgos Coustakis had imagined she'd bought with her gleaming gold store card, all she was going to appear for dinner wearing was a chainstore skirt and blouse. But suddenly she stopped dead.

The racks were full, weighed down with plastic-swathed clothes.

'What—?'

'Kyrios Coustakis ordered them to be purchased for you, *kyria*. They were delivered just now by a personal shopper. There are accessories and lingerie as well,' said the maid's softly accented voice behind her. 'Which dress would you like to wear tonight?'

'None of them,' said Andrea tightly. She reached for the hanger carrying her own humble skirt and blouse.

The maid looked aghast. 'But...but it is a formal dinner, tonight, *kyria*,' she stammered. 'Kyrios Coustakis would be very angry if you did not dress appropriately...'

Andrea looked at the maid. The expression on the girl's face made her pause. There was only one word for the expression, and it was fear.

She gave in. She could defy her grandfather's anger, but she was damned if he would get the chance to terrorise one of his own staff on her account.

'Very well. Choose something for me.'

She went and sat back on the bed while the girl leafed through the clothes hanging from the rail. After a few moments she emerged with two, deftly removing the protective wrapping from them and laying them carefully across the foot of the bed. Andrea inspected them. Both were clearly very expensive, and although it was the short but high-necked cocktail length one that she preferred for style, she nodded at the other one, a full-length gown.

'That one,' she said.

It was emerald-green, cut on the bias, with a soft, folding bodice and a long, slinky skirt. Andrea found her hand reaching out to touch the silky folds.

'It is very beautiful, *ne*?' said the maid, and sounded wistful as well as admiring.

'Very,' agreed Andrea. She glanced at the girl. 'I don't know your name,' she said.

'Zoe, *kyria*,' said the girl.

'Andrea,' she replied. 'And I don't believe in servants.'

Some twenty minutes later, staring at herself in the long mirror set into the door of the closet, Andrea was stunned.

She looked—fantastic! That was the only word for it. The dress was a miracle of the couturier's art, its soft folds contrasting with the rich vividness of its colour. True, the bodice, held up by tiny shoestring straps, was draped dangerously low over her full breasts, encased in a fragile, strapless bra, but she had to admit the effect was very…well, *effective*! It gave the dress the finishing touch to the 'wow' impact it made.

She had scooped her hair up into a knot on her head, with tendrils loosening around the nape of her neck and gracing her cheeks and forehead, and she'd redone her make-up to match the impact of the dress.

With a final look at her reflection, she turned and headed towards the door, where the manservant who had come to summon her stood waiting. Staff though he was, she could see the admiration in his eyes. For an instant, in her mind's eye, it was not one of the house staff who stood there, but the man she had encountered on the terrace that afternoon, looking at her with those powerful grey eyes, making her stomach give a little skip…

She bestowed a slight, polite smile on the manservant, and headed towards the curving marble staircase.

It was time to go into battle once more…

Nikos Vassilis stepped on the accelerator, changed gear and heard the powerful note of the engine of the Ferrari change pitch. He was not in a good mood. Twice in one day now he'd made the journey out of Athens at the behest of Yiorgos Coustakis. Tonight was not a good night to be dining with the old man. He'd planned a leisurely evening with Xanthe, whose petite, curvaceous body was, he had discovered, a pleasant alternative to Esme Vandersee's greyhound leanness. Xanthe was proving very attentive—she was clearly keen to take his mind off Esme Vandersee, and was now pulling out all the stops to renew Nikos's interest. Which meant, he mused, that she was coming up with some very interesting ideas indeed to do so...

A smile indented his mouth. Last night with Xanthe had been very enjoyable—she had seen to that. Ah, he thought pleasurably, there was nothing like a Greek woman for making a man feel good! Yes, Esme Vandersee might be eager for him, he was certainly a catch for her, but as an American she suffered that infernal affliction of thinking that a woman had a right to give a man a hard time if she chose! Usually, of course, any petulance that Esme displayed he disposed of very swiftly— she was as sexy as a cat and getting her horizontal soon improved her mood...

But even so, he mused, Xanthe understood what it was that a man wanted a woman to be. And she made it obvious that she was keen to be so very attentive to his every need....

His smile vanished. Well, he'd be kept waiting tonight before availing himself of Xanthe's rediscovered charms! Yiorgos Coustakis was obviously taking considerable pleasure in jerking his strings—just for the hell of it, it seemed. Their meeting that afternoon, ostensibly to discus the technicalities of reversing Vassilis Inc into Coustakis Industries, had hardly been urgent, and could have been left to their respective finance directors to sort out. But obviously Old Man Coustakis had relished getting Nikos Vassilis to come traipsing out of Athens to that overblown villa of his whenever he snapped his fingers.

Thinking about the afternoon meeting brought another image vividly to mind—that of Yiorgos Coustakis's flame-haired mistress.

Nikos's mouth tightened. The woman had been so blatant, and so unashamed of what she was doing at the Coustakis villa. Not to mention eyeing him up and trying her wiles out on him to boot!

Mind you, Nikos thought, had the woman not been tainted by her distasteful association with a man old enough to be her grandfather, then her approach to him might well have got a warmer welcome.

Considerably warmer, in fact...

An image of her dark auburn hair floating around that perfect face, the way her breasts had thrust against the material of her jacket, played in his memory. Oh, yes, she was worth remembering, all right! Her beauty was so flamboyant, so eye-catching, that almost—almost he had been tempted to overlook just for whose benefit it had been paraded that afternoon. Not for him—for a seventy-eight-year-old man.

He thrust her memory from him. However alluring the woman, she was beyond the pale so far as he was concerned.

He revved the engine again, enjoying the superb handling of the extortionately expensive car beneath his hands. Driving a high-performance car like this was like having sex with a high-performance woman...they were both so extraordinarily responsive to his touch...

His mind snapped away from the analogy. For the next few hours, until the ordeal of a tedious, overlong dinner with Yiorgos Coustakis was done with, he had better keep his libido under control.

Think of your bride, Nikos!

That sobered him all right. It was about time Old Man Coustakis brought the girl out from wherever he had her stashed. She would know all about her intended bridegroom by now, no doubt, and she and her mother were probably already waist-deep in wedding plans. Presumably the girl wanted a lavish society wedding. Well, he didn't care one way or the other, and, since the whole purpose of marrying her was to seal his acquisition of Coustakis Industries, the more high-profile the better! After all, he had nothing against the girl—let her have her extravagant wedding if she wanted. Once she was his wife it would be *her* who would have to fit herself around what *he* wanted—that was what Greek wives did. Oh, he would be generous, of course, and considerate to her position—he had no intention of making a bad husband—but he did not envisage changing his life a great deal on account of the Coustakis heiress.

Pity she was obviously so plain... The thought of having a

sexually desirable, docile and attentive wife had its attractions, now he came to think of it.

He braked the Ferrari in front of the security-guarded gates of the Coustakis villa, presented his credentials, and moved on down the drive at a speed greater than he would normally. He wanted this evening over and done with.

CHAPTER FOUR

NIKOS stood in the ornate salon, itching for dinner to be announced. His host seemed to be in no hurry. He was regaling his guest with a lengthy description of his latest toy—a one-hundred-and-fifty-foot yacht which he had just taken delivery of. It was, by all accounts, an opulent vessel, and Yiorgos was telling him in great detail about the splendour of the décor of its interior—and how much it had all cost. The telling seemed to be putting him in a good humour. His colour was high, but his eyes were snapping with satisfaction.

'And you, my friend,' he said, slapping Nikos on the back with a still powerful hand, 'will be the first to try her out! You will spend your honeymoon on it! What do you think of that, eh?'

Nikos smiled briefly. Again, a honeymoon spent on board Yiorgos Coustakis's new yacht would send just the message to the world he wanted.

'Good, good,' said his grandfather-in-law-to-be, and slapped him once more on the back. Then his head snapped round. Automatically Nikos followed his gaze. A servant had opened the double doors to the salon.

A figure stepped through.

It was the flame-haired temptress!

Nikos felt a kick to his gut that was as powerful as it was unwelcome.

What the hell was she doing here?

The woman had paused for a moment in the doorway—*making sure all eyes were on her*, Nikos thought—and now started to glide forward towards them. Her head was held high—that glorious dark auburn hair twisted up into a topknot that revealed the perfect bone structure of her stunning face.

As for the rest of her…

Nikos felt his breath catch again. The dress was simply breathtaking on her, revealing the lushness of her figure even more generously than the close-fitting jacket had that afternoon. Now, instead of only being able to imagine the rich creaminess of her skin, he could see acres of it displayed for him, from her swan-like neck down across the sculpted beauty of her shoulders, the graceful curve of her bare arms and, best of all, towards the swell of her ripe breasts…

He felt himself ache to caress them…

Like a chill breath on the back of his neck, he felt Yiorgos Coustakis watching him. Watching him lust after his mistress.

Disgust flooded through him. Whatever the hell the old man was playing at, bringing his mistress to dinner, taking pleasure in seeing his guest responding to her lavish charms, he would have none of it! His face hardened.

For Andrea, walking in through the doors and then freezing to a stupefied halt at seeing the very man she had been trying not to think about all evening standing there beside her grandfather, it was like *déjà-vu* all over again. Just as the first sight of her had brought instant sexual appreciation into the man's eyes, so, an instant later, that had been replaced by disdain—all over again.

And, just as she had on the terrace, she reacted instinctively. Her chin went up; her eyes glinted dangerously.

She was glad of her anger—it took her mind off the fact that her heart was racing like a rocket and that her eyes were glued to his face.

She stopped, resting her hand on the back of an antique sofa beside her. Her eyes met those of the stranger, defiant and glittering.

'Well,' said Yiorgos Coustakis to the man he had chosen to be his son-in-law, 'what do you think of her?'

What the hell do I say? thought Nikos savagely. He said the only thing he could.

'As ever, Yiorgos, you have impeccable taste. She is…outstanding.'

They were speaking Greek, Andrea registered. Well, of course they would be! Her eyes flew from one to another.

'You are to be envied,' Nikos went on, with gritted politeness, wondering what the hell to say to the old man about the woman he was warming his bed with. Disgust was filling his veins. He wanted out of here—fast.

Yiorgos Coustakis smiled.

'I give her to you,' he said. He made a gesture of presentation with his hand. The satisfaction in his voice was blatant.

Nikos froze. *What the hell was this? Was this supposed to be some kind of sweetener that the old man imagined he might want in order to bed his plain, sexless granddaughter?* If so, he had better extricate himself from the delusion.

'Your generosity is…overwhelming, Yiorgos,' he managed to get out. 'But I cannot accept.'

A look of deliberate astonishment lit Yiorgos Coustakis's face. 'How is this?' he demanded. 'I thought…' He paused infinitesimally, milking the pleasure he was getting from the situation to its utmost, watching this arrogant, ambitious pup squirm for one moment longer. 'That you *wanted* my granddaughter? That you were impatient to meet her…'

He gave a short laugh, his eyes snapping with malicious pleasure as he watched Nikos's face change expression as the truth dawned.

'She is my granddaughter, Nikos—what did you imagine, eh?' he asked softly.

Only Nikos's years of self-discipline enabled him to keep his expression steady. Inside, it felt as if the floor had given way beneath him.

'This is your granddaughter?' he heard himself say, as if seeking confirmation of the unbelievable.

Yiorgos laughed again, still highly pleased with the joke he had played on the younger man. He knew perfectly well what conclusions he had jumped to when, just as Yiorgos had planned, he had first set eyes on the girl that afternoon, sublimely unaware that the plain-faced fiancée he had been led to expect was no such thing at all.

He glanced across at the girl and beckoned imperiously.

'Come here,' he commanded in English.

Andrea walked forward. Her heart was pounding again. She could feel it thrilling in every vein. The man with the steel-grey eyes was looking at her full on, and she was all but knocked senseless by the way he was looking at her—either that or jolted by a million volts of electricity scorching through her.

If she'd thought he'd looked a knock-out that afternoon, in his hand-made business suit, the way he looked now, in his tuxedo, simply took her breath away! She swallowed. This was ridiculous! No man should have such an effect on her! She'd seen good-looking blokes before, been eyed up by them—even kissed some in her time—but never, *never* had any man made her feel like this.

Breathless, terrified—enthralled. *Excited!*

Beside the man, her grandfather ceased to exist. She took in a vague impression of a stockily built figure, shoulders bowing with age, and that craggy, heavy-featured face she had registered as he'd sat at his desk that afternoon.

But right now she had no eyes for him.

She was simply drinking in the man at his side—she wanted to stare and stare and stare.

'My granddaughter,' said Yiorgos.

Nikos hardly heard him. The entire focus of his attention was on the woman in front of him. *Theos*, but she was fantastic! Was she really the Coustakis girl? It couldn't be possible. Then, with a fraction of his brain that worked, he realised that the old man had set him up deliberately—leading him on to think that he was going to be shackled to a plain wife, when all along...

He smiled. Oh, what the hell—so the old man had set him up! He didn't care! Hell, he could even share the joke! A sense of relief had flooded through him, he realised, and something more—exultation.

Yes! That woman, that fantastic flame-haired temptress, was *not* out of bounds after all. In fact—his smile deepened—she was very, very within bounds...

Andrea saw the smile, brilliant, wolfish, and felt her stomach lurch. Oh, good grief, but he was something all right! She felt the breath squeeze from her body.

Nikos reached and took the girl's hand. He lifted it to his mouth. Andrea watched the dark head bend as if in slow motion. She still couldn't breathe, her lungs frozen as she felt the long, strong fingers take hers.

Then even more sensation laced through her. He was brushing her fingers with his lips. Lightly, oh, so lightly! But oh, oh, so devastatingly. A million nerve endings fired within her, like the *whoosh* of a rocket cascading stars down upon her head.

As he raised his head he smiled down at her.

'Nikos Vassilis,' he said, and looked right into her eyes.

His voice was low—the tone intimate.

She stared up at him, lips parted. She could say, or do, nothing.

'Andrea—'

The word breathed from her. She could hardly speak, she found.

'Andrea...' His voice echoed her name, deeper than her husky contralto. 'It is good to meet you.'

He let his eyes linger on her one last, endless moment, then, tucking her hand into the crook of his arm, he turned to his host.

'You're an old devil, Yiorgos,' he said with grating acknowledgement. 'But in this instance the joke was worth it.'

Andrea's eyes flew between them—the language was back to Greek. What was going on? Then, suddenly, Nikos turned back to her.

'Come, let me take you through to dinner.' His voice was warm, and the caress in it made her nerve-endings fire all over again. That and the over-powering closeness of him, her hand caught in his arm. She felt she ought to pull away from him— but for the life of her she could not.

As if in a dream she let herself be escorted from the room, across the vast entrance hall, and into a grandiose dining room.

With the utmost attentiveness this most devastating man, Nikos Vassilis—*Who is he?* she found herself wondering urgently—drew back her chair, waving away the manservant who came forward to perform the task, and settled her in her seat.

She wanted to glance up and smile her thanks politely, but she could not. Shyness suddenly overwhelmed her. This was like something out of a fairytale—she dressed like a princess, and he, oh, he like a dark prince!

Instead she mumbled a thank-you into her place-setting.

As he took his place opposite her—only one end of the long mahogany table was occupied, with Yiorgos taking the head and his granddaughter and her fiancé on either hand—Nikos felt a deep sense of well-being filling him.

He couldn't have asked for a more beautiful bride! Old Man Coustakis was doing him proud. Oh, he would never have been unkind, even to a plain wife, but having that flame-haired beauty at his side, in his bed, was going to make married life a whole, whole lot sweeter for him!

He glanced across at her. She was still staring at her place-setting as if it was the most interesting thing in the room, but she was aware of him all right. Every male instinct told him that. But if she were behaving as a well-brought-up young girl should—showing a proper shyness in the face of the man she was to marry—well, who was he to complain?

A memory of the way she had boldly walked up to him on the terrace, her voice husky as she sought to introduce herself, intruded, conflicting with the image of the meekly downturned head opposite him. A frown flickered in his eyes. Then it cleared. She must have seen the look he had given her then and been angered by it—and rightfully so! No gently reared female would care to be taken for such a one as he had first thought her. Well, now that misunderstanding was out of the way it would not trouble them again.

Another frown flickered in his eyes. The girl was English,

that was obvious—both by her colouring and her use of the language, quite unaccented.

As the manservant drew forward to start serving dinner Nikos glanced at his host.

'You did not tell me that your granddaughter was half-English, Yiorgos,' he opened. He spoke in Greek, and as he did he noticed Andrea's head lift, her eyes focus intently on him, concentrating.

Yiorgos leant back in his chair.

'A little surprise for you,' he answered. His eyes gleamed.

Nikos let his mouth twist. 'Another one,' he acknowledged. Then he turned his attention to Andrea.

'You live in England? With your English mother?' he asked politely, in Greek. That must be the reason she had addressed him in English this afternoon.

Andrea looked at him. She made as if to open her mouth, but her grandfather forestalled her.

'She does not speak Greek,' he said bluntly. He spoke in English.

Nikos's eyes snapped together. 'How is this?' he demanded, sticking with English.

'Let us say her mother had her own ideas about her upbringing,' said Yiorgos.

Andrea stared at her grandfather—just stared. Then, as if knowing exactly why she was staring, he caught her eye. Dark, intent. Warning.

His words echoed in her mind from the afternoon. *You will be on the first plane back to London unless you do exactly,* exactly, *what I want you to do!*

She felt her blood chill. Was going along with some fairy story he wanted to tell this guest of his about her upbringing part of that imprecation? What do I do? she thought wildly. Open my mouth and set the record straight right away?

And achieve what, precisely?

She knew the answer. Get herself thrown out of her grandfather's house and sent back to London without a penny for her mother. And she wouldn't go home empty-handed; she *wouldn't*! She would get Kim the money she deserved, whatever it took. Even if it meant colluding with Yiorgos Coustakis's attempt to whitewash his behaviour.

So she buttoned her lip and stayed silent.

From across the table Nikos saw her expression, saw the mutinous gleam in those lustrous chestnut eyes. So, the girl had been brought up in England, by a mother who had her own ideas, had she? Ideas that included depriving the Coustakis heiress of her natural heritage—the language of her father, the household of her grandfather. What kind of mother had she been? he wondered. An image presented itself in his mind—one of those sharp-tongued, upper-class, arrogant Englishwomen, expensively dressed, enjoying a social round of polo and house-parties at one stately home after another. He frowned. Why had she married Andreas Coustakis in the first place? he wondered. Doubtless the marriage would not have lasted, even if Yiorgos's son had not been killed so young. He found himself wondering why Yiorgos had so uncharacteristically let the widow take his granddaughter back to England with her, instead of keeping her in his household. Well, his generosity had been ill-paid! Now he had a granddaughter who could not even speak his own language!

I could teach her...

Another image swept into his mind. That of this flame-haired beauty lying in his arms as he taught her some of the more essential things that a Greek bride needed to be able to tell her husband—such as her desire for him...

He let his imagination dwell pleasantly on the prospect as they began to dine.

Through his long lashes, Nikos watched with amusement as Andrea began to eat appreciatively. Though he was pleased to see her take evident sensuous delight in fine food—Esme's gruelling diet had always irritated him, and Xanthe was picky about what she ate as well—he would have to keep an eye on his bride's appetite. At the moment she could get away with hearty eating—her figure was lush and queenly, and she carried no surplus pounds at all, he could tell—but if she continued to put food away like that for the next twenty years she would be fat by forty! A thought struck him. How old was she, exactly? When he'd first set eyes on her he'd taken her for twenty-five or so, but surely Yiorgos would not have kept her unmarried for so long? She must be younger. Probably her English mother and that sophisticated aristocratic society she doubtless enjoyed had served to make her appear more mature than she really was.

Yet another thought struck him, less pleasant. If she'd been brought up in England just how sure could he be that she was coming to him unsullied? English girls were notoriously free with their favours—every Greek male knew that, and most of them took advantage of it if they got the chance! Upper-class English girls were no longer pure as the driven snow—some of them started their sexual lives at a shamefully early age. Could she still be a virgin? He thought of asking Yiorgos out-right, but knew what the answer would be—*Do you care enough to walk away from Coustakis Industries, my friend?*

And he knew what his own answer to that would be.

Virgin or no, he would marry Andrea Coustakis and get Coustakis Industries as her dowry.

Eating the delicious dinner—there seemed to be an endless ar-ray of courses—served to take Andrea's mind a fraction off the man opposite her. But only by a minute amount. Then, just as she was beginning to calm, he started talking to her.

'What part of England do you live in, Andrea?' he asked her civilly, clearly making conversation.

'London,' she replied, daring to glance across at him briefly.

'A favourite city of mine. Your life there must be pretty hectic, I guess?'

'Yes,' said, thinking of the two jobs she held down, working weekends as well as evenings, putting aside every penny she could to help pay off those debts hanging over her mother. Kim worked too, in the local late-night-opening supermarket— neither of them got much time off.

'So what are the best clubs in London at the moment, do

you think?' Nikos went on, naming a couple of fashionable hot-spots that Andrea vaguely recognised from glossy magazines.

'Clubbing really isn't my scene,' she answered. Not only did she get little free time to go out, but the kind of nightlife available in her part of London was not the kind to feature in glossy magazines. Anyway, dancing was out for her, and Kim had brought her up to appreciate classical music best.

'Oh,' replied Nikos, realising he felt pleased with her answer. Clubbing was strongly associated with sexual promiscuity, and he found himself reassured by her answer. 'What is your "scene", then, Andrea?'

She looked at him. Presumably he was just making polite conversation to his host's granddaughter.

'I like the theatre,' she said. It was true—the biggest treat she could give Kim, and herself, was to see the Royal Shakespeare Company, visit the National Theatre, or go to any of the great wealth of other theatres London had to offer. But tickets were expensive, so it was something they did not indulge themselves in often.

Nikos named a couple of spectacular musicals running in the West End currently—obviously he was no stranger to London, Andrea thought. She shook her head. Tickets for such extravaganzas were even more expensive than for ordinary theatre.

'I prefer Shakespeare,' she said.

She could tell, immediately, she had given the wrong answer. She glanced warily at her grandfather. His eyes had altered somehow, and she could sense his disapproval focussing on her. Now what? she wondered. Wasn't it OK for her to like Shakespeare, for heaven's sake?

She got her answer a moment later.

'No man likes a woman who is intellectually pretentious,' the old man said brusquely.

Andrea blinked. Liking Shakespeare was intellectually pretentious?

'Shakespeare wrote popular plays for mass audiences,' she pointed out mildly. 'There's nothing intellectually élite about his work, if it isn't treated as such. Of course there are huge depths to his writing, which can keep academics happy for years dissecting it, but the plays can be enjoyed on many levels. They're very accessible, especially in modern productions which make every effort to draw in those who, like you, are put off by the aura surrounding Shakespeare.'

Yiorgos set down his knife and fork. His eyes snapped with anger.

'Stop babbling like an imbecile, girl! Hold your tongue if you've nothing useful to say! No man likes a woman trying to show off!'

Astonishment was the emotion uppermost in Andrea's re-action. She simply couldn't believe that she was being criticised for defending her enjoyment of Shakespeare. Automatically, she found herself glancing across at Nikos Vassilis. Did he share her grandfather's antediluvian views on women and their 'intellectual pretensions'?

To her relief, as she met his eye she realised that there was a distinct gleam of conspiratorial humour in it.

'So,' said Nikos smoothly, coming to the girl's rescue after her grandfather's reprimand, 'what is your favourite Shakespeare play?' He ignored the glare coming from his host at his continuing with a line of conversation he disapproved of.

Andrea ignored it too, glad to find her grandfather's dinner guest was more liberal in his expectations of female interests.

'*Much Ado About Nothing,*' she replied promptly. 'Beatrice and Benedict are my favourite hero and heroine! I just love the verbal warfare between them—she always answers back to every jibe he puts on her, and never lets him put her down!'

The humour vanished from Nikos's eyes. A bride with a penchant for a heroine specialising in verbal warfare with her future husband was not his ideal. However stunning her auburn looks, he found himself wishing that the Coustakis heiress was all-Greek after all. A pure Greek bride would never dream of taking pleasure in answering her husband back!

Andrea saw his disapproval of her choice, and her mouth tightened. Nikos Vassilis might be a drop-dead smoothie, but scratch him and he was cut from the same metal as her grand-father, it seemed. Women were not there to be anything other than ornamental and docile.

She gave a mental shrug. Well, who cared what Nikos Vassilis thought women should be—let alone her grandfather? She wasn't here to win the approval of either.

She went back to eating her dinner. Across the table, Nikos was distracted from thinking further about the woman he had elected to marry by Yiorgos peremptorily asking his opinion on some aspect of global economic conditions. Clearly he had heard quite enough from his granddaughter. It was obviously time for her to revert to being ornamental and docile. And silent. Knowing nothing about global economic conditions, only a great deal about her straitened personal ones, Andrea tuned out.

Then, after the final course had been removed—and she felt as if she could never look another rich, luxurious dish in the face again—her grandfather abruptly pushed his chair back.

'We will take coffee in the salon, after I have checked the US markets,' he announced. He looked meaningfully at Nikos as he stood up. 'Join me in twenty minutes.'

He left the dining room. Nikos glanced after him, then back at Andrea.

'Even at his age he does not relinquish his mastery, not for a moment,' he said. He sounded, thought Andrea, almost approving.

'Surely he's got enough money,' she said tartly.

Nikos, who had got to his feet as the older man had risen, looked down at her.

'Easy to say that,' he observed evenly, 'when you have lived in luxury all your life.'

She stared at him. Again, astonishment was uppermost in her breast. Was this more of her grandfather's fairytale at work? She said nothing—Nikos Vassilis was the dinner guest of the man who was going to fund her mother's removal to Spain. Baring her family's unpleasant secrets to him was unnecessary.

He came around to her side of the table and held out his hand, a smile parting his lips. 'Come,' he said. 'We have been given twenty minutes to ourselves. Let us make the most of them.'

Thinking that the company of Nikos Vassilis was a good deal more bearable than that of her grandfather—even if he clearly didn't like her approving of Shakespeare's feisty heroine Beatrice!—Andrea went along with him. He escorted her, hand tucked into the crook of his arm again—a most disturbingly arousing sensation, she rediscovered—from the dining room, opening large French windows to emerge out on to the same terrace where she had first seen him that afternoon. After the brightness of the dining room the dim night outside made her blink until she got her night vision. She glanced up.

The night sky was ablaze with stars. Though it was early summer still, the air was much warmer than it would have been in England. She gave a little sigh of pleasure and walked forward, disengaging herself to place her hands on the balustrade and look out over the dim gardens.

All around in the darkness she could hear a soft chirruping noise.

'What's that?' she asked, puzzled.

'You would call them by their Spanish name, I think—cicadas,' said Nikos behind her. He had come up to her and was, she realised, standing very close to her. It made her feel wary, and something more, too, that made her heart beat faster. 'They are like grasshoppers, and live in bushes—they are the most characteristic sound of the Mediterranean at night.' He gave a frown. 'Surely you have heard them before?' he asked.

Whether or not she had been brought up in England, it was impossible to imagine that a girl from a background as wealthy as hers would not be well-travelled, especially in fashionable parts of the Mediterranean.

She shook her head, not really paying him much attention. Cicadas—so that was what they sounded like. She remembered how her mother, when Andrea was just a little girl, asking after the father she had never known, had sat on her bed and told her, her soft voice sad and happy at the same time, how she had walked along the sea's edge, so many years ago, hand in hand with the man she loved, heard the soft lapping of the Aegean, the murmurous sound of cicadas in the vegetation. Her heart squeezed—*Oh Mum, why did he have to die like that?*

'What are you thinking of?' Nikos asked in a low voice as his fingers drifted along the bare cusp of her shoulder.

That the touch of your fingers is like velvet electricity...

'Just someone I think about a lot,' she answered, trying to make her voice sound normal when every nerve in her body was focussed on the sensations of his skin touching hers.

Why is he touching me? He shouldn't! He's only just met me!

She wanted to move away, but she couldn't.

'A man?' There was the slightest edge in his voice, but she didn't hear it. She was only aware of the drift of his fingers on her bare shoulder.

'Yes,' she said dreamily.

His hand fell away.

'What is his name?' The question was a harsh demand. She turned, confused. Why was he angry? What on earth made him think he had any business being angry? Was it just because an unmarried Greek girl shouldn't think of men?

'Andreas,' she answered tightly. As she spoke she found herself noticing that anger, though it shouldn't, seemed to have sharpened his features into bold relief. He looked, though she shouldn't think it, even more gorgeous.

'Andreas? Andreas who?'

She lifted her chin. Whatever right this complete stranger seemed to think he had subjecting her to an inquisition, she answered him straight.

'Andreas Coustakis,' she bit out. 'My father.'

He was taken aback, she could see.

'Your father?' His voiced echoed hollowly. He nodded his head stiffly. 'My apologies.' He paused. 'You knew him?'

She shook her head. Her throat felt tight. He must have

walked on this very terrace, she suddenly thought. Known this house. Stormed from it the night he was killed…

'No. But my mother…tells me of him…'

Nikos heard the betraying husk in her voice. It struck a chord in him deeper than he had thought possible. He, too, had never known his father. Never even known who he was…

And his mother had never talked of him, except to say that he had been a sailor on shore leave. From a northern clime. Given his son's height, a Scandinavian, perhaps? She hadn't known. Hadn't cared.

Andrea's mother had cared. Cared enough to tell her daughter about the father she had never known.

A shaft of envy went through him.

'What does she tell you?' he heard himself asking.

Was it the soft Aegean night? Andrea wondered. The kind, concealing blanket of the dark that made her feel, suddenly, that she could tell this man anything—that he would understand?

'She tells me how much she loved him,' she answered, her eyes skimming out into the darkness of the gardens below, lit by the stars above. 'How he loved her, so dearly. How he called her his sweet dove—how he would lay the world at her feet…'

Her voice broke.

'And then he died.' The sob sounded deep in her throat. 'And the dream ended.'

Tears pricked in her eyes. Blinding her vision. Blinding her senses. So she did not feel his arms come around her, turning her into him, folding her head upon his chest so that the tears might come.

'Hush,' he murmured. 'Hush.'

For a long, timeless moment she let herself be held by this man, this complete stranger, who had shown her so unexpectedly the kindness of strangers.

'I'm sorry,' she mumbled. 'I think it's being here, in the house he lived in, and realising how real he once was.'

She pulled away from him, but he caught her elbows so she could not back away completely.

'Don't be ashamed to weep for him,' he said to her quietly. 'You honour him with your tears.'

She lifted her face to his. The tears gleamed on her lashes like diamonds beneath the starry heavens. Her soft mouth quivered.

He could not help himself. Could not have stopped himself if an earthquake had rumbled beneath his feet.

His mouth lowered to hers. Caught her sweetness, her ripeness. His hands slipped from her elbows, around her slender back, pulling her in towards him.

She gave a soft gasp, and it was enough. His tongue slipped between her parted lips, tasting the nectar within. He moved his mouth slowly, but, oh, so sensuously on hers, and he felt her tremble in his arms.

A rush of desire flooded through him. She was exactly how he wanted her to be. Her body ripe in his arms, her mouth tender beneath his.

He deepened his kiss, his hands as of their own volition sliding down her back to shape the rich roundness of her bottom.

Sensation whirled through Andrea. She felt as if she was melting against him, her body moulding to his, and her mouth—oh, her mouth was like a flower, dissolving in sweetness.

Warm shivers ran through her body. She couldn't think, couldn't focus on anything, anything at all, except the sensations flooding through her veins, liquid, honeyed, sweeping her away, drowning her in desire.

And then, with a rasp of reality, she surfaced, pulling away from him. She was shocked, trembling.

'No—' The denial breathed from her, eyes distended. Heart pounding.

What was she denying? she thought wildly. Denying his helping himself to her? Denying that a moment's brief human comfort had suddenly been transformed into a sensuousness so overwhelming she was reeling with it?

Or more? Denying—and her stomach clenched as she faced

up to what she was really denying—denying that never, ever in her whole life had she ever dreamt it was possible to feel such sensations...

He had not let her go, she realised. Although she had pulled away, he was holding her still, his hands in the small of her back. She was arching back, away from him, totally unaware of how the gesture thrust her breasts towards him, making him ache to bend his head and touch his mouth to their swollen fullness, aroused, all against her knowledge, to crested peaks.

'No—' she breathed again. Her hands came up to the corded strength of his arms and tried to dislodge them.

He felt the pressure on them and released her immediately, though it went against every primal instinct, which was to keep her close against him, closer still, press her warm, ripe body against his, moulding her to him, feeling every rich curve, every soft, delicious inch of her...

Theos, but he wanted her! Wanted her with an urgent aching that was nothing, he realised, nothing at all like the controlled, detached sexual desire that he felt for Esme, or Xanthe—or any other woman he had ever bedded, he realised with a shock.

Was it because this woman here, now, was to be his bride, his wife? Was it the primeval emotion of bonding, cleaving, that had released something in him he had never known existed?

Until now?

A rush of fierce possessiveness surged through him. It was like a revelation. He had never felt possessive about his women before—had always known that for them he was just one more male, just better-looking, richer—or both—than most of the men they took to their beds. Exclusivity, on either side, was not a word applied to the relationships he had enjoyed. He knew perfectly well that Esme Vandersee had a whole court she picked her lovers from, depending on her whim and their availability in her hectic globe-trotting life. And Xanthe—well, he was not the only man keeping her in the luxury she enjoyed so much. Of course she was skilful enough, tactful enough, never to let her lovers catch a glimpse of each other, but Nikos could have named a handful of wealthy Athenians who enjoyed her carefully disposed favours.

It didn't bother him.

Not like the thought of Andrea Coustakis thinking about another man...

The rush of possessiveness intensified. It was as alien as it was heady, and he gave himself to it totally.

Then, as the rush consumed him, he realised that he was going too fast—much too fast. Too fast for him—and certainly too fast for her.

His eyes focussed on hers.

She was standing, backed against the balustrade, still close enough for him to reach and pull her to him, but he did not. The expression in her eyes stopped him.

They were shocked, staring.

For a moment exultation speared him. She felt the same way he did! As if a revelation had suddenly made her see the world in a completely different way. Then, with a sobering recognition, he realised that her reaction to what had just happened was more complex than his.

More fearful.

'Andrea,' he said softly, 'don't be alarmed. I'm sorry—I'm rushing things too much.' A wry smile tugged at his mouth as she stared at him, half of her mind drinking in the male beauty of his face, the other still too shocked to take in anything at all. 'You must blame your beauty,' he told her. 'It is too lovely to resist.'

She shivered. He fancied her, and so, on the briefest acquaintance imaginable, he had pounced on her?

'Don't look at me like that,' he said ruefully. 'I will not touch you again until you want me to. But you must not blame me—' the tug of wry humour came again to his well-shaped mouth in a way that did strange things to her insides '—if I try very hard to make you want me to touch you again...'

He stepped back a pace, giving her more space.

'Come,' he said and his breath was more ragged than he

preferred, 'take my hand, if nothing else, and let us talk a while. We have, after all, much to talk about.'

He took her hand, and she let its cool strength curl around her fingers and draw her away from the balustrade. They began to head down towards the far end of the terrace at a leisurely pace. The night air fanned Andrea's heated face and gave her a moment's breathing space.

But her mind was racing as fast as her heart!

What was she doing out here on a starlit terrace with a man who took her breath away, who had casually kissed her as she had never been kissed in her life?

A man she didn't even know.

But who had promised to make her want him touch her again...

What was it he had said? she wondered. *'We have, after all, much to talk about.'*

Puzzlement suffused her. Was that some kind of Greek pick-up line? Or was he simply trying to take the pressure off her and make polite chit-chat again?

She looked up at him as they walked.

'Why have we got so much to talk about?' she asked. Her voice was still husky, even though she did not mean it to be. It was also puzzled.

He glanced down at her. His lashes were extraordinarily long, she found herself thinking irrelevantly. It made her completely miss what he said in answer.

Except for one word.

She stopped in her tracks.

'Say that again,' she said. Her breathing seemed to have stopped.

Nikos smiled down again at her, his eyes warm.

'I said, my sweet bride-to-be, that perhaps we should start by talking about our wedding.'

Andrea's breathing stopped totally.

CHAPTER FIVE

IT WAS as if, in front of his eyes, she had changed. Like some alien shape-shifting from a harmless creature into some terrifying monster.

She thrust her hand from him, backing away, freezing as she did so.

'Our *what*?'

'Our wedding,' he repeated. His voice was tighter now, automatically responding to the visible rejection her whole body was projecting.

She was staring at him as if he had grown another head.

'Our *wedding*?' She could hardly get the word out. Then, as terror seized her, she found her voice. Only a frail one. 'Oh, my God,' she breathed, as the only possible truth dawned, 'you're some kind of lunatic—'

She swirled around, catching at the narrow skirt of her dress, forcing her legs—weak, suddenly—to hurry back along the stone terrace towards the lights—the safety—of the open French windows at the other end.

He caught her wrist before she could even take a single frantic step.

'*What* did you call me?'

The circle of his strong fingers crushed her bones. She tugged to free herself, but to no avail.

'Let me go!' The fear was naked in her voice now, her eyes wide with panic.

His face darkened. 'What the hell is going on?' he demanded. 'I simply said we ought to discuss our wedding—I am quite prepared to give you as free a hand as possible, but I have to say,' he went on, still at a loss to account for the bizarre reaction he was getting from her, 'I would prefer to be married here in Greece.'

'*Married?*' She echoed the word with total incredulity.

'Yes, married. Andrea, why on earth are you behaving like this?' There was impatience in his voice, as well as bewilderment.

'Married to *you*?'

His mouth thinned. It was the way she said that, as if it was the most outrageous idea in the world. He glared down at her.

He let her hand go abruptly. She rubbed her wrist, and would have tried to bolt to the doors leading inside, but he was blocking her back against the stone balustrade.

'We need to talk,' he said abruptly.

Andrea shook her head violently. The only thing she needed to do was to get inside, away from this lunatic who had suddenly gone nuts and started talking about weddings and getting married...

'Answer me,' he commanded. 'Why did you let me kiss you just now if you did not believe that I would marry you?'

Her heart was plummeting around all over the place inside her. Panic was nipping at her, ready to explode again at any moment. Now it did.

'Oh my God, you are completely nuts!' She tried to push past him, but he was an immovable block.

Nikos, not moving an iota, gave a heavy, impatient sigh and tried hard to hold on to his patience. Why she was throwing this fit of hysterics was incomprehensible. Could it really be that she did not know about their marriage? How could that possibly be? Of course she knew! She *must* know! So why the hysterics now?

Did she not *want* to marry him?

The thought enraged him suddenly! How dared she lead him on as she had this evening, letting him taste the sweetness of her lips, inflaming his desire with the allure of her body, if she did not agree to their marriage? And why should she not agree? What, if you please, was so very wrong about the idea of being his wife?

Perhaps because you are the bastard son of a barmaid and an unknown sailor?

The poisonous root took hold and would not be shaken loose. His jaw tightened. If she had objected to their marriage on those grounds she had had time enough to make her opinions clear to her grandfather.

And was Yiorgos Coustakis the kind of man to listen to his granddaughter's objections about the social origins of her intended husband?

He thrust the thought from him. It was irrelevant. Right now he simply had to stop her throwing a full-scale fit of hysterics.

'Be still. You are not going anywhere until you have calmed down—'

His words were cut off by a sharp expletive as he registered pain in his shins. Then, as he was caught off-balance, Andrea thrust him back with all her strength and hurtled as fast as her evening dress would allow towards the open doors at the end of the terrace.

Pain forgotten, Nikos surged after her and intercepted her at the threshold to the dining room.

'Enough!' He was angry now. His hands closed over her shoulders and he gave her a brusque shake. 'Behave yourself! There is no need for such a ludicrous reaction to what I have said!'

As he spoke, it dawned on Nikos that that was what was angering him most of all—her instant and total rejection of the notion of marrying him! He found it intolerable! Here he was, having steeled himself for the past couple of weeks to doing the unthinkable—marrying at all, and to a complete stranger—and then finally, tonight, to have all his worries so deliciously and unexpectedly set aside by seeing just what a peach the Coustakis heiress actually was...and here she was having a fit of hysterics over it! As if the prospect of marrying Nikos Vassilis was the most repellent in the world!

Andrea arrowed her hands and forearms up between his and jerked them sideways with a violent movement to free herself.

Her heart was pounding now—panic, disbelief and above all hot, boiling anger was pouring through her.

She could not believe what she had just heard—couldn't *believe* it! It couldn't be true! It just couldn't!

Her face twisted. 'This is some kind of joke, yes? Talking about me marrying you! Some idiotic, warped idea of a joke, right?'

Nikos bristled. A joke, the idea of marrying him? A fatherless bastard raised on the streets of Athens? His face darkened. He looked scary suddenly, she realised.

'You are the Coustakis heiress,' he said coldly. 'I am the man who will take over the company when your grandfather retires. What else but we should marry?'

'The Coustakis heiress?' Andrea echoed in a strange voice. A laugh escaped her. High-pitched. Distorted. She took a deep, shuddering breath. 'Let me get this right. You, Mr Vassilis, want to marry me because I am Yiorgos Coustakis's granddaughter and you want to run his company for him—is that it?'

He assented with a brief, glancing nod of his dark head. 'That is so. I am glad you understand.'

Completely missing the ironic tone of his voice, she took another breath—a tight one this time. 'Well, sorry to disappoint you, chum, but it's no go. You'll have to find yourself another heiress to marry!'

She made to turn away. She felt in urgent need of escape, not just into the villa, but up to the sanctuary of her own room.

An arm barred her way in.

'You are offensive.'

The voice was soft, but it raised the hairs on the back of Andrea's neck.

She turned back slowly. Nikos Vassilis was very close. Far too close.

'*I* am offensive? Mr Vassilis, you are a guest in my grandfather's house and I suggest you start remembering your responsibilities in that role.' She spoke in as forbearing a manner as possible, which was extremely taxing in the circumstances.

'I make due allowance for the different customs in Greece, but if you imagine that kissing me on a terrace somehow converts instantly into a proposal of marriage you are living in the Middle Ages! You have *not*, I do assure you, compromised me into marrying you! So you can just forget all about blackmailing my grandfather into marrying me off to you just because I was stupid enough to fall into your arms like a...like an *idiot*!'

Her anger was with herself as much as him. This was what came of letting herself be swept away by a drop-dead gorgeous stranger on a starlit terrace! He suddenly got ideas of catching himself a rich wife. A sudden, inexplicable stab of pain went through her as she realised that that was all the kiss had meant to him—it had been nothing to do with *her*, just a cheap way to entrap the girl he thought was Yiorgos Coustakis's heir!

The Coustakis heiress he had called her! Hysterical laughter threatened in her throat. God, it might almost be worth indulging his insane pretensions just for the joy of seeing her grandfather's reaction when he demanded marriage to save the 'honour' of the offspring of a woman he'd called a slut to her face—and her daughter's!

'Blackmail?' The word ground out. Furious outrage seared in Nikos voice. To have his behaviour likened to that of Yiorgos Coustakis when he had forced his father-in-law's hand to get his daughter and her dowry was insupportable. 'How dare you make such an accusation!'

Andrea threw back her head. 'What else should I call it? Sliming around after me like a dog sniffing out a bone! Well, let me tell you something, Mr Vassilis—my grandfather will laugh in your face at the idea of your marrying me to get hold of Coustakis Industries!'

The scorn in her voice enraged him.

'You are mistaken.' His voice was icy. 'It was his idea in the first place.'

She stilled.

'Are you saying—' her voice was choked '—that my grandfather is in on this?' Her insides were hollowing out all over again. 'My *grandfather* wants me to marry you?'

'What else?' Could it really be that she did not know? That Old Man Coustakis had not bothered to tell his granddaughter what his plans were? Another of his 'little jokes', Nikos thought grimly to himself.

'Let me get this straight.' Andrea's voice was controlled. 'My grandfather wants *me* to marry *you*—'

'In exchange for my taking over Coustakis Industries when he retires, which will be shortly after our marriage. It is all agreed between us,' Nikos elucidated. He felt in no mood to spare the girl's feelings any more. Her reaction to the discovery of their betrothal was insult enough to warrant his spelling out the financial grounds of their marriage very, very clearly.

'How very convenient.' Her voice was flat. And still very, very controlled.

'Is it not?' agreed Nikos. The irony was back in his voice.

Disbelief washed over Andrea, wave after wave. Total disbelief at what she had heard. She felt quite faint with it. Then, deep, deep inside, she felt the waves break upon some hard, immovable bedrock.

'Excuse me—'

She moved past Nikos Vassilis. The man who had just told her that her grandfather—her dear, kind grandfather, who had ignored her existence all her life—had plans for her. Marriage plans.

Marriage!

She had thought Nikos Vassilis insane, and assumed he was just chancing it. But his assumptions were based on something much, much more solid than a soft, seductive kiss...

As she walked across the dining room she could feel the rage mounting. Misting over her eyes like a red miasma. She marched through the double doors into the wide, marble-floored hallway and strode across, flinging open the doors to the library.

At her entrance her grandfather looked up from the bank of

computer screens flickering on the console drawn up beside his mahogany desk.

'Out!'

The order was given imperiously. She ignored it. She surged forward.

'This man,' she burst out, gesturing wildly behind her to where Nikos had paused in the doorway, following her dramatic entrance, 'has announced that he will be marrying me! I want you to tell him *right now* that it's not going to happen!'

Her grandfather's face had hardened.

'You heard him correctly. Why else would I send for you? Now, leave—you are disturbing me.'

The sick hollowness caverned in Andrea's stomach.

'Are you completely out of your mind?' Her voice was hard—hard, and trembling with fury. 'Are you completely insane—to bring me here, spring this on me and think I'd go along with it? What the *hell* do you think you're playing at?'

Yiorgos Coustakis got to his feet. He was no taller than his granddaughter, but his bulk was considerable.

And suddenly very, very formidable.

Almost she faltered. Almost she quailed beneath the look of excoriation on his lined, powerful face. But rage carried her forward.

'You must be *mad* to think you can do this! You must be completely ma—'

Her denunciation was cut short. A look of blinding fury flashed across Yiorgos Coustakis's face.

'Be silent!' he snarled. 'You will not speak in such a fashion! Go to your room! I will deal with you in the morning!'

She stopped dead.

'Excuse me?' Her eyes were wide with disbelief. 'You think you can give me orders? I am not one of your hapless lackeys!'

'No, you are my granddaughter, and as such I demand obedience!'

Andrea's mouth fell open.

'Demand away,' she told him scornfully. 'Obedience isn't a word in my vocabulary.'

Behind her, Nikos's eyes narrowed. He was witnessing, he knew, something that very few people had ever seen—someone standing up to the vicious, domineering and totally ruthless head of Coustakis Industries.

For a brief, fleeting second Andrea could see by the expression in her grandfather's heavy hooded eyes that he had *never* been spoken to in such a fashion. Then, swiftly, his face hardened into implacable fury at her defiance of him.

'You will leave this room now or I will have you removed! Do you understand?'

He jabbed his finger at an intercom button on his desk and snarled something into the speaker in Greek. Then he turned his attention back to Andrea.

She was in front of the wide desk now, adrenaline running in every vein. She was simply too furious to be frightened. Besides, deep down in her consciousness she knew that if for a moment she gave in to her grandfather, let herself be cowed by him, it would all be over. He would have won and she would have been reduced to a terrified, intimidated wreck. Just the way he had terrified and intimated her mother. Well, he was not going to do the same to her! No way! It was essential, absolutely essential, that she outface him.

And she had every right to be angry—every right! The very idea that he had been discussing marriage...*marriage!*...at all, let alone behind her back like this, was so appalling she could hardly believe it to be true. It couldn't be true! It just couldn't!

'I'll go when I'm ready!' she bit at him. 'When you tell me that this lunatic you invited here is out of his mind!'

She had enraged her grandfather all over again.

'Silence! You will not shame me in my own home, you mannerless brat! And you will not speak of your betrothed husband like that!' The flat of his hand slammed on the surface of his desk to emphasise his anger.

Andrea's eyes widened with shock. 'You don't mean that,' she said. 'You don't seriously mean that. You can't! Tell me this is some kind of idiotic joke the two of you are playing!'

Yiorgos Coustakis's face was like stone.

'How dare you raise your voice to me? Why do you think you are here? You are betrothed to Nikos Vassilis and will marry him next week. Anything else is not your concern! That is an end to it! Now, go to your room!'

Faintness drummed at her. This was unreal. It had to be. It just had to be...

'You can't *possibly* have brought me here for such an outrageous idea,' she said. Her breathing was heavy, heart pounding in her chest. 'It's the most insane thing I've ever heard in my life! And *you* must be insane to think I'd go along with it!'

Somewhere, behind her, she could hear a sharp intake of breath. She didn't care. A whole lot of anger was coming out now—twenty-five years' worth of anger against the man who had behaved so unforgivably to her mother. She owed him nothing—nothing at all.

And as for this insane idea of his...

Her grandfather was standing up, coming out from behind his desk. His face was almost purple with anger.

The blow to the side of her head sent her reeling. She gasped with the pain and the shock, unable to believe that she had just been struck. Automatically she stepped back, almost tripping in her long tight skirt, raising her right forearm into a blocking gesture.

'Go to your room! This instant!' snarled Yiorgos Coustakis again. His eyes cut into her like knives.

Lowering her guard by merely a fraction, Andrea thrust her head forward. 'If you ever hit me again I'll send you flying, so help me! You're a vile, callous *bastard*, and you don't push me around, not *ever*, so get that through your head right now!'

'Get out of here!' A stream of vituperative Greek poured out of Yiorgos Coustakis's mouth.

She took a deep, shuddering breath. 'I'm going. Don't worry! But before I go,' she said, her jaw tight with controlled rage, 'you had better understand something! I am *not* some pawn, some patsy for your vile machinations! The very *idea* that you seriously thought you could marry me off like some *chattel* is so ludicrous I can't *believe* you even entertained it for a second! So go take a hike, Yiorgos Coustakis!'

She saw his hand lift again and threw her arm back up to block him just in time. The blow landed on her arm-bone, jarring it painfully, but it had shielded her face.

She screamed, in shock, rage, pain and horror, and then suddenly her left arm was being taken in a grip she could not shake off, her right arm forcibly lowered from its blocking position.

'Enough—'

Nikos's voice was harsh and imperative. It was directed at both of them.

Yiorgos's face was contorted, eyes alight with a viciousness that would have scared her had she not been so overwhelmed. Then his eyes shot past her, towards the door. Two men were standing there, deferentially awaiting further orders. Nikos's head swivelled around to look at them. Security guards.

'Get her out of here,' Yiorgos Coustakis instructed them curtly. His breathing was heavy, his colour dangerously high. The two men started towards Andrea.

'Stop.' Nikos's voice held the note of command and it stopped the men in their tracks.

Andrea twisted in Nikos's unshakeable grip, taking in the uniformed men. Her eyes had widened yet again, in even greater disbelief.

'This is not necessary, Yiorgos,' said Nikos tightly.

'Then *you* get her out,' growled his host. 'And you had best take a whip to her to control her! She needs a good beating!' He raised his hand again, as if he would start the process himself, and willingly.

'You *bastard*!' spat Andrea at her grandfather.

Nikos jerked her backwards, turning her around to get her out of the room.

She went. Getting away from that vile, ugly scene was suddenly the most urgent thing in the world. As she was frogmarched out she tried to shake herself free.

'Let me go! I'm getting out of here!'

As they entered the hallway, the two security guards stepping smartly aside to let them pass, Nikos released her.

'You little savage! What were you thinking of, behaving like that? Do you run so wild you can't have a civil discussion without yelling your head off?'

Her eyes flared.

'He hit me! He *hit* me and you defend him?'

Nikos, exasperated, gave a sharp intake of breath. 'No, of course I do not defend him, but—'

The two security staff walked by, heading back to their own quarters. Nikos waited till they were out of earshot. He knew the type. Utterly professional, utterly incurious. They would do the bidding of their employer, whatever orders they were given. Manhandling a young woman upstairs to her bedroom would have been a piece of cake for them.

A thought struck him and he called out after the men as they were about to disappear. Old Man Coustakis had looked fit to have a seizure—him dropping dead right now would be highly inconvenient.

'Send Kyrios Coustakis's valet to him—he may need attention.'

One of the men paused and nodded, then went off with his companion. Nikos glanced back at the woman he had agreed to marry for the sake of Coustakis Industries. His mouth tightened.

Andrea was holding the back of her hand to her reddened cheek. Her own colour was high, irrespective of the blow she had taken. *Theos*, she had obviously inherited the old man's temper, thought Nikos. What a termagant!

An immense sense of exasperation overcame him. What the hell was he doing here, stuck in the middle of a battle between Old Man Coustakis and his spitting she-wolf of a granddaughter? Why the hell couldn't the old man have sorted it out first with the girl, telling her about the husband he had chosen for her instead of letting him get caught in the cross-fire like this?

He needed a drink. A strong one. Perhaps that would calm the girl down as well.

She was still trembling with anger. His frown deepened. Her ear and cheek were still red where Yiorgos's hand had impacted.

He tilted her face into the light. 'Let me see.'

She brushed his arm aside, and jerked free. 'Don't touch me!' she spat.

She was still in complete meltdown, chest heaving, stomach churning, adrenaline going crazy inside her.

'You need a drink—it will calm you down.' He spoke grimly.

He took her elbow again, and this time Andrea let herself be led back into the drawing room. She collapsed down on a silk-upholstered sofa while Nikos went to raid the antique inlaid drinks cabinet. He returned with two generous measures of brandy.

'Drink,' he ordered, handing Andrea one of the glasses.

She took a sip, finding her hands were shaking. The fiery liquid seemed to steady her, and she took another sip. Across the room Nikos was standing, his expression closed and moody, one hand pushing back his tuxedo jacket, resting on the waistband of his trousers. Absently she noticed the way the white lawn shirt showed the darker shading of chest hair, the way the material stretched across toned pecs and abs.

She dragged her eyes away and rubbed again at her stinging cheek. She was in shock, as well as everything else, she knew.

I've got to get out of here, she thought wildly. She would leave, first thing in the morning, and head back to London. To home, to sanity.

It was the only thing to do.

She still couldn't take it in. Couldn't believe it.

'Is it true? Tell me?' She heard the question burst from her.

Nikos frowned.

'That you and he have hatched some idea of me…me marrying…marrying you?' She could hardly get the words out.

'Yes.' Nikos's voice was terse. Dear God, what an unholy mess! 'I had thought,' he went on, openly sarcastic, 'that you had just obtained irrefutable corroboration from your grandfather?'

Her face hardened.

'That bastard!'

Nikos's expression iced. He had no love for Coustakis—he doubted if anyone in the world did, now that his poor besotted wife was dead!—and certainly he should not have hit her, but Andrea must be stupid indeed if she did not realise that her grandfather would not tolerate her shouting defiance at him, let alone in front of another male, and her selected husband to boot! Yiorgos Coustakis would never permit himself to lose face in front of the man he had accepted would run the empire he had amassed. Moreover, whatever his faults, Andrea should be mindful of the fact that it was Yirogos's money that kept her in her luxurious lifestyle, and that she owed him courtesy, if nothing else.

'You will not use such language.'

'Or what?' she spat. 'You'll take a whip to me like he told you to?'

Nikos swore. He wanted out, right now. He wanted to be miles from here, away from this madhouse! The thought of Xanthe Palloupis hovered tantalisingly in his mind. She would be soft, and warm, and soothing, and cosseting. She would sit him down and make him comfortable, and relaxed, and speak only when he wanted her to speak, and never say a word otherwise, would know instinctively, from long practice, what he wanted, what he did not want...

But he wasn't with Xanthe; he was listening to this redheaded hot-head spitting venom.

'You certainly need *something* to stop you behaving like a foul-mouthed spoilt brat!' he barked back at her.

She got to her feet. 'I suggest you leave, Mr Vassilis,' she said. 'And I also suggest, next time you get around to thinking of marrying someone, you have the courtesy to ask her first before announcing a done deal! However much you want to get your greedy hands on Coustakis Industries, I'm not available—especially not to some pretty-boy fortune-hunter like you!'

She slammed the brandy glass down on the sideboard, not caring that the liquid slopped on to the marquetry surface, spun on her heel and stormed out of the room, clattering up the marble staircase to get to her room as soon as she could.

Behind her, Nikos's face was rigid with fury. Ten seconds later he was out of the house and gunning his Ferrari down the driveway as if possessed by demons.

Andrea's fingers were trembling as she punched the buttons on the mobile phone Tony had leant her. Reaction had set in with a vengeance, and she felt as weak as a kitten.

The conversation was brief and to the point—if for no other reason than she did not want to run up Tony's phone bill more than she had to.

'Tony—it hasn't worked out. I'm going to have to come home. Tomorrow. Don't worry.' She swallowed, not daring to let herself start on what had happened. 'It's nothing drastic, but I'm just going to come home anyway. OK?' She paused fractionally. 'Look, if you don't hear from me from Athens airport tomorrow, go on yellow alert, will you? And if I don't show up at Heathrow—or, worse, don't phone tomorrow evening— go to red, OK? I've met my beloved grandfather and he's—' she swallowed '—running to type.'

After she'd hung up, desperately grateful not only to have heard Tony's familiar calming voice, but also just to have been reminded that a sane, reasonable world existed outside the confines of this palatial madhouse, Andrea realised her hands were still trembling.

How she managed to get any sleep at all that night she didn't know. She awoke late in the morning, with a jolt, woken by Zoe gently shaking her shoulder. Her grandfather, it seemed, wished to see her. Immediately.

Oh, does he? Well, as it happens, I want to see him as well! To order a car to take me to the airport!

He was in his bedchamber, Andrea discovered as, grim-faced, hastily dressed in a cheap blouse and cotton trousers of her own, she followed the maid along the corridor. With clammy hands she walked into the room.

Her grandfather was sitting up, propped on an array of pillows, ensconced in a huge tester bed that would not have looked out of place in Versailles. He did not look well, Andrea registered, and for the first time she realised that he was an old man not in the best of health.

I'll do this civilly, she thought. *I can manage that if I try.*

She approached the foot of the bed. Dark, hooded eyes bored into her. Yiorgos Coustakis might be confined to his bed, but the power he could wield had not lessened an iota.

'So,' he said heavily, 'you are worse than I ever feared. Insolent beyond belief! I should have taken you from your slut of a mother and raised you myself! You would have learned proper respect from the back of my hand!'

Every good intention vanished from Andrea's breast instantly. She felt the fury surge in her veins. But this time she would not lose control.

Instead she simply stood there, looking at the man who had fathered her father. It seemed unbelievable that they should be related in any way.

'Silent at last! A pity you could not have held that hellish tongue of yours last night, instead of showing yourself up so abominably in front of your husband!'

'Nikos Vassilis is not my husband, and he never will be,' replied Andrea. Her anger was like ice running in her blood.

Yiorgos Coustakis made a rasping sound in his throat.

'And you could whistle for him now! No man would touch you after witnessing your despicable display last night! But then—' his dark eyes filled with contempt '—without Coustakis Industries as your dowry you would be fit only to warm a man's bed for hard cash, like your whore of a mother!'

'This conversation,' said Andrea, her voice as tight as a drawn bowstring as she tamped down the fury that filled her as she heard this vile man speak so of her mother, 'is pointless.

I am leaving for London. Be so good as to order a car to take me to the airport.'

Yiorgos Coustakis's dark face suffused with colour.

'You are going nowhere! You will stay in your room until the morning of your wedding if you take that attitude with me! I will be master in my own house!' His fist slammed down on to the bedcovering. 'And if it takes something more than incarceration to bring you to heel, then so be it! A good beating will turn you docile!'

Andrea paled. A memory of those two expressionless security staff sprang into her mind. Fear stabbed at her. He saw it, and smiled. Her blood chilled as she saw him.

'Hah! Do you think I wouldn't? I thrashed your father with my belt often enough! He soon learnt obedience!' His face darkened. 'Until he met the whore who gave you birth! Then he defied me! I sent him packing! He would have got not a penny from me—if he hadn't smashed himself to pieces in his hurry to get back between the slut's legs!'

She felt the horror of it as if it had been yesterday. Her father, terrorised and abused by this foul man who had caused such misery, and then, just when happiness was at last within his reach, to have it all snatched from him—even his life.

'You vile, vile man…'she whispered. 'You're not fit to live.'

The dark, soulless eyes scorched through her. 'Get out, before I take my belt to you myself! I will not be defied by you—or anyone!'

'Oh, I'm going,' said Andrea. 'If I have to walk into Athens on foot, I'm going!'

His face contorted.

'You will not be allowed to step foot outside this house until Nikos Vassilis takes you off my hands!'

She shook her head. 'You are mistaken. I am leaving—today.'

'From inside a locked room? I think not!'

Andrea looked at him steadily. Now was the time to make things clear to him.

'That,' she said, her eyes like stones, 'would be unwise. You

see, if I don't make a certain phone call every night, the British
embassy in Athens will be alerted that I am being held against
my will. You will not, I am sure, wish to be charged with
imprisoning me! Let alone invite the feast the press will make
of it!'

The effect of her words was visible. He spat something at
her in Greek. She smiled scornfully.

His face contorted. 'And if I *make* you make that phone
call?'

The threat was open—and quite plain to understand.

'Oh, that would be unwise too. You see—' she smiled un-
pleasantly, hiding the shudder that had gone through her at his
words '—if that should happen then I might give the wrong
code word during the conversation...'

As if a shutter had dropped, her grandfather's face suddenly
became completely unreadable. There was nothing there—none
of the fury and temper that had been blazing from him a moment ago.

'Tell me,' he said suddenly, 'if you please, just why is it
that you are so averse to the prospect of marrying Nikos
Vassilis?'

His change of tack took her aback. Then she rallied. 'Is that
a serious question? It's too absurd to be worth asking!'

'Why? Is he not a fine man to look at? He would make a
handsome husband, *ne*? His reputation with your sex, I understand—' his voice became sly '—is spectacular! Women flock
to him, and not just because of his money!'

'Money?' Andrea caught at the word. 'He's a fortune-hunter!
He admitted as much.'

Yiorgos Coustakis gave a harsh laugh. 'He seeks to net a
greater fortune, that is all! Do you imagine I would entrust my
empire to someone untried and untested? Nikos Vassilis has
his own fortune—he will not waste mine by incompetence and
mismanagement!'

She frowned, trying to take in this turnabout. Her grandfather
went on. 'Vassilis Inc is capitalised at over five hundred million
euros! He's been after a merger with Coustakis Industries for

the last eighteen months—he's an ambitious man, and now, finally, I have decided to let him realise his ambitions.' His voice hardened. 'But I've driven the price higher—he has to marry you before I sign the deal.'

Andrea's brain was racing, trying to make sense of what she was hearing.

'Why?' she said bluntly. 'You've denied my existence for twenty-five years, ever since your goons forced my mother to the airport and shoved her on a plane back to England!'

Nothing showed in his face, not a trace of regret or shame, as she related the way Yiorgos Coustakis had disposed of the woman who had dared to tell him she was pregnant by his dead son.

'Why?' Yiorgos Coustakis echoed. 'Because you carry my blood. You and no one else. I have no choice but to use you, tainted though your blood is. When you marry Nikos Vassilis he will guard my fortune, and my blood will pass through you to your son. He will be my heir. I have had to wait two generations, but I shall have my heir!'

There was a fierceness of possession in his eyes that even his inscrutable expression could not disguise.

So, thought Andrea, as his words sank in, this is what it's all about. I am the vessel for his posterity. Revulsion filled her. Yiorgos Coustakis was nearing the end of his misbegotten life and he wanted the only immortality he could find.

She looked at him. He had everything money could buy, but as a human being he was worthless. He had no kindness in him, no compassion, no gentleness, no feeling for anyone except himself. He had treated his own son like a possession to be beaten into obedience, and her mother had been instantly condemned as a gold-digger trying to get at his precious money!

And now, twenty-five years later, she was standing in front of him, knowing that she was the only person in the world who could give him what he wanted. The final thing he wanted.

The memory of Tony's voice echoed in her mind. *Look, if*

he does want you for something, then if he doesn't want you to refuse he's going to have to do something you *want.*

And there *was* something she wanted. Something she had travelled over a thousand miles to get—the money for her mother that was not just her escape to the sun but her reparation as well. Justice. Finally.

Her grandfather's eyes were resting on her. Seeing her as a tool to be used. Nothing more. Her heart hardened. Well, tools had to be paid for.

Five minutes ago she had wanted nothing except to shake the dust of her grandfather's house from her feet. Now she wanted to get what she came for.

Money.

His shoulders relaxed into the pillow as he read her mind.

'So,' he said, 'tell me—what price do you set on opening your legs to Nikos Vassilis with a ring on your finger to keep you respectable?'

The sneer in his voice was irrelevant. So was the insult and the crudity. Everything about him was irrelevant—except the money he would pay her. Her heart was hard, like stone all the way through. Somewhere in the back of her mind a memory was flickering—the memory of being held in strong arms, her body on fire with soft, seductive flame...

She thrust it away. That kiss had been nothing to do with her. Nikos Vassilis had kissed her because she was the gateway to Coustakis Industries. No other reason. She just hadn't realised it at the time. Now that she did she must not read anything more into it. Nothing.

'Five hundred thousand pounds,' she announced crisply. 'Sterling. Paid into a bank account in London of my choosing, in my name—Andrea Fraser.'

She gave her mother's surname—her name—deliberately. She was no Coustakis. Never had been. Never would be.

His laugh was derisive. 'You set a high price on yourself for the daughter of a penniless slut!'

Nothing showed in her face. She would not allow it.

'You need me. So you'll pay for me. That's all.'

A flash of fury showed in his eyes. 'Do you think that as the wife of Nikos Vassilis you will live the life of a pauper? You will live in a luxury you can hardly dream of! You should be grateful, *grateful*—on your knees that I have plucked you out of your slum to live such a life as I am offering you!'

'Five hundred thousand.' Her voice was implacable. She needed that much to clear the last of Kim's debts, buy her a decent apartment in Spain, and have enough left over to invest safely for an income for her mother to live on, albeit modestly, for the rest of her life. 'Or I go back to London today.'

Dark eyes bored into hers. She could see the hatred in them. The loathing that this tool he wanted to use was daring to defy him. But defy him she would—she had something he wanted, and he would have to pay for it. Just as Tony had said.

But he would not go down easily.

'You get not a penny until you are married.'

She laughed scornfully. 'There will be no marriage,' she said as her eyes narrowed, 'unless I am paid.'

Even as she spoke her mind was splintering in two. What was she doing here? What was she thinking of, selling herself like this? She must be mad! Quite mad!

But then the other side of her mind slammed back. This was no time for scruples, no time for doubts! It was now or never—this was her one and only chance to get reparation for Kim. She would do whatever it took! And agreeing to marry a total stranger was what it was going to take.

A stranger who can melt your bones in a single embrace? Oh, be careful—be careful of what you are doing!

Compunction flashed at her. She was standing here, negotiating a price to marry Nikos Vassilis as if she were doing nothing more than haggling over a CD at a car-boot sale! How low was she stooping?

Then her heart hardened again. And hadn't Nikos Vassilis stood in front of Yiorgos Coustakis and negotiated a price to get hold of Coustakis Industries? A price that included marriage to a woman he'd never set eyes on? What kind of man did that?

No, she need feel no shame, no compunction. The man who had kissed her last night deserved no more regard than did her grandfather!

For one long, last moment she held her grandfather's eyes, refusing to back down. It was too important to even think of giving in. At last, after what seemed like an eternity of challenge, he suddenly snarled, 'On your wedding morning—and not till then! Now, get out!'

CHAPTER SIX

NIKOS sat in his boardroom, lounging back in his leather chair at the head of the table, listening to his directors droning on about the impact of the merger with Coustakis Industries. He wasn't listening. Wasn't paying the slightest attention. His heart was stormy.

What the hell kind of woman had he agreed to marry? A raging hell-cat! A spoilt brat of a pampered princess! An ill-mannered, ill-tempered, badly behaved harpy who threw tantrums and hysterics at the drop of a hat! A true Coustakis!

His jaw tightened. The last thing on earth he needed was a wife who took after Yiorgos Coustakis!

A splinter of grudging admiration stabbed him. The girl hadn't flinched from confronting Old Man Coustakis. She'd just stormed in there and laid in to him!

A smile almost curved his mouth at the recollection. *Theos*, but it had been a sight to see. Someone giving as good as they got from that vicious brute whose ugly reputation made most people walk on tiptoes around him, from house servants to business associates. Even he trod carefully around the old barracuda! At least until Coustakis Industries was his to run.

The smile turned to a frown. For all that, however, it was not behaviour to condone. Certainly not in the woman who would be Mrs Nikos Vassilis. It was unthinkable that his wife should behave like that—for whatever reason!

The frown deepened—but from a different cause this time. Had the girl truly not known of her grandfather's marriage plans for her? It was typical of Yiorgos Coustakis not to bother himself with trivial details such as telling his granddaughter what husband he had chosen for her. In which case, Nikos knew he had to acknowledge, the girl had a right to object to

having been kept in the dark about such an important matter.
True, her reaction had been wildly over the top, but in the first
immediate shock of the news it was understandable that she
should be affronted at her grandfather's typically high-handed
behaviour in keeping her ignorant of her future.

An image flashed in his mind. Yiorgos Coustakis slashing
his hand down across Andrea's cheek. Nikos straightened suddenly in his chair. Anger clenched at him. *Theos*, but the old
man was a brute! Who cared if he was from a generation that
thought nothing of beating children? Who cared if his granddaughter had provoked him by yelling like a harridan in front
of the man he had chosen for her husband? No man ever hit a
woman. Ever.

Revulsion filled him. Whilst he would never dream of raising
his fist to a man of Yiorgos's age, the memory of him hitting
his granddaughter burned.

I've got to get her out of there!

A surge of emotion swept through him—not anger with that
brute of an old man. Something he had never felt about any
woman before. A fierce, urgent burst of protectiveness.

Abruptly he lifted a hand, cutting off whatever his sales di-
rector was saying.

'Gentlemen, my apologies, but I must leave you. Please continue with the meeting.'

Ten minutes later he was in his Ferrari and nosing through
the impossibly jammed streets of Athens. Heading out of town.

Andrea sat out on the terrace overlooking the ornate gardens
that spread like an embroidered skirt around her grandfather's
opulent villa. Her heart was heavy—but resolved. The final
scene with her grandfather replayed itself over and over again
in her head. Was she insane, even to contemplate going along
with what he wanted? This wasn't just some kind of trivial
business contract she had agreed to—this was *marriage*!

The enormity of what she committed herself to overwhelmed
her, making it seem almost unreal. So much had happened so
quickly! Less than two days ago she had been at home, in her

own drab but familiar world. Now she was sitting on a sun-drenched terrace beneath a Mediterranean sun—about to marry a complete stranger!

Panic rose in her throat and she fought it down.

It's not a real marriage! It's just a wedding ceremony. That's all. The day after the wedding I'll be on a plane to London! My 'husband' will be glad to see the back of me!

And I'll have half a million pounds waiting for me in the bank!

She and Kim could be in Spain, house-hunting, in a month!

The warm sun poured down on her, bathing her legs stretched out in front of her. They had been aching since last night—wearing high heels was never a good idea—and the strain and tension of the past day and a half was telling. Gently she stretched and eased them, rubbing her hands lightly along her thighs in a careful massage.

The warmth did them good, she knew. Living in Spain would help. She would get work there, enough to keep Kim and herself, so that Kim could take life easy at last. Spain was full of Brits now; she was bound to be able to get some kind of job, even if she didn't speak Spanish yet.

I'll invite Tony and Linda for a holiday she thought happily. They'd been so good to her; it would be great to give some-thing back. She'd had to phone Tony from her room, just a short while ago, telling him she was staying after all. It had taken quite a lot to convince him she really meant it, that one of her grandfather's bully-boys hadn't been twisting her arm to say so!

Cold filled her. Her grandfather was unspeakable—her every worst fear about him was deserved! He really would have thought it perfectly acceptable to keep her a prisoner here and force her into marrying that man!

That man—

Memory leapt in her throat. It was here, on this terrace, that she had first laid eyes on him, not twenty-four hours ago. Here, beneath the beguiling stars, that he had slid her into his arms and kissed her…

I'm going to marry him...

A shaft of pure excitement sliced through her. She felt a quickening inside herself. That man, that drop-dead, fabulous-looking, breathtaking man, whose touch had set fire to her, melting her very being into him, Nikos Vassilis, was going to be her husband...

Reality hit like a cold douche. Of course he wasn't going to be her husband! Not for more than a day! All he was to her was her passport to Spain with her mother, nothing more!

And all I am to him is his passport to my grandfather's money!

Her lips pressed together. What kind of man was he that would even think of marrying a woman he'd never laid eyes on just to get hold of an even bigger fortune than he yet had? That he wasn't even a fortune-hunter somehow made it worse! Being poor herself, she knew how tempting it must be to think that you could claw your way out of poverty the easy way. But if Nikos Vassilis was already rich, had already made his pile, then why did he want even more? If his company really was worth five hundred million euros then a fraction of what he already possessed would have kept her and Kim in luxury by their standards!

Well, it was none of her business. She didn't care about Nikos Vassilis. He was using her to get what he wanted—and she was simply returning the favour! And she wasn't even cheating him. Even after she'd been packed off home he'd still have got what he wanted—Coustakis Industries—courtesy of his brand-new and totally unwanted wife! He'd be perfectly happy if the bride didn't stick around like glue! A grim smile played about her mouth. In fact, the only person who would end up with a bad bargain would be her beloved grandfather! He'd have handed over his company to Nikos Vassilis, along with his despised granddaughter, but he'd be waiting a long time for his precious heir!

The throaty roar of a high-powered car approaching the house along the long drive that was hidden from the front gardens interrupted her bitter reveries. She tensed. It did not sound like the purr of the huge limousine her grandfather had taken his leave in some half-hour ago—heading, she assumed for his office in Athens. This was a much more aggressive engine in-deed—and it didn't take a genius to guess whose it was.

Some few minutes later her assumption was confirmed. Nikos Vassilis strode out on to the terrace. He came to where she was sitting.

Andrea felt her body tense. Something leapt inside her. He was looking spectacular again. A pale grey immaculately cut business suit, gleaming white shirt, grey silk tie, made him look taller and more svelte than ever. His expression was unread-able, made more so by the dark glasses covering his eyes, and as she looked at his face she felt her stomach hollow out.

Oh, dear God, he's just gorgeous! she felt herself thinking.

He sat himself down opposite her, stretching out his long legs, his feet almost touching hers. Automatically she drew her legs back, the sudden movement causing a jolt of mild pain to go through them.

He caught the expression on her face and frowned slightly

'Are you all right?'

The rich timbre of his voice, so seductively accented, made her feel weak. She nodded briefly to answer his query, unable to speak.

'How is your cheek?'

The frown had deepened, and before she could stop him he had reached across the table and touched the side of her face with his fingers. They felt cool, but where they made a thou-sand sensations quiver through her. He tilted her head slightly, so that he could see where he touched.

There was a bruise, definitely, even if only faintly visible. She had made no attempt to cover it with make-up, though she had let her hair fall loose, so that it covered her right ear which was still red from having caught the main thrust of her grand-father's blow.

'Fine,' she said quickly, brushing his hand aside. She did not want his concern—the last words she had flung at him had been an atrocious insult, and his evident concern for her now put her off kilter. So did the echoing resonance of his light velvet touch just now…

The soft-footed approach of a servant carrying a tray of coffee for two was a welcome interruption. It gave Andrea precious moments to collect herself.

Nikos lifted off his dark glasses and slid them into his breast pocket. Andrea wished he hadn't. Although it was disturbing to address a man whose eyes she could not see, it was far, far worse to have those keen slate-grey eyes visible to her.

The eyes searched her face.

'You are upset still,' he said quietly. 'Last night was very distressing for you. I apologise—it should not have happened that way.' He paused, feeling carefully for his words. 'Your grandfather is a…difficult…man, Andrea, as you must surely already appreciate from all your years of knowing him. He is used to commanding others, to giving orders—and to getting his own way by the swiftest means possible. However brutal.' There was a frown in his eyes. 'Hitting you was insupportable. But—' he held up a hand to ward off what her reply must be '—understandable. That is not to excuse him, Andrea—merely to point out that there was no way he was going to be outfaced by his own granddaughter in front of me, and that he comes from a generation which did not believe in sparing the rod.'

Andrea stilled. She thought of her father, brought up here, a vulnerable boy, bullied by his father from the day he was born—thrashed into obedience…

The only bright hope of his life had been Kim, the girl he'd met on a beach and fallen in love with on the spot, their young romance an idyll out of *Romeo and Juliet*. And just as doomed.

I'm not just doing this for you, Mum—I'm doing it for my father too. Looking after you the way he was never able to…

Nikos Vassilis was talking again. She forced herself to listen.

'You must believe me when I tell you that last night I naturally assumed you knew of your grandfather's marriage plans for you—and agreed to them.'

She reached forward to the coffee pot—filter coffee, she noticed gratefully, not the treacly Greek brew—and started to pour them both a cup.

'But I do agree to them,' she announced. 'I've had a talk with my grandfather this morning and it's all settled, Mr Vassilis. You can continue with your merger plans.'

Her voice was remarkably calm, she thought. But then that was the way to play it—cool, calm and collected. This was not a real marriage they were talking about; it was part of a business contract that would benefit them both. She must remember that and not think about anything else.

Certainly not about the way the sensual line of his mouth contrasted with the tough, cleanly defined edge of his jaw, or the way his dark silky hair made her long to reach her fingers to it...

She pushed the cup towards him.

'Milk and sugar?' she asked politely.

He shook his head briefly, a frown creasing between his eyes.

'Did he bully you again?' he demanded openly.

Her eyes widened in surprise.

'Certainly not,' she answered, economising on the truth to cut to the chase. 'We struck an excellent deal that I'm perfectly satisfied with.'

She poured milk into her coffee and took a reflective sip.

'Deal?' There was an edge in Nikos's voice that Andrea would have had to have been deaf not to hear. 'What deal?'

She smiled. It was an artificial smile, but for all that she could not stop a curl of satisfaction indenting her mouth. Satisfaction that at last, after a quarter of a century, her mother would get reparation from Yiorgos Coustakis. Devastated, heartbroken and pregnant, Kim had asked nothing from Andreas's father, had wanted only to offer him and Andreas's mother the comfort of knowing that, although their son had died so tragically, a grandchild had been conceived. She had not asked for money—she had offered comfort and consolation.

But Yiorgos Coustakis had treated her like a gold-digging whore...

'Finally, Mr Vassilis, I get money of my own.'

'Money?' There was a chill in his voice now that raised the hairs on her neck, but she kept the tight, artificial smile pasted to her lips.

'Yes, money, Mr Vassilis. You know—the crisp folding stuff, the bright shiny stuff, the silent, electronic stuff that wings its way into bank accounts and makes the world go round.'

Her eyes were bright and hard.

'Explain.'

That was an order, just as if Nikos Vassilis had been speaking to one of his underlings. And if he owned a company worth five hundred million euros, Andrea reminded herself deliberately, that meant he had one hell of a lot of underlings!

'Explain? Well, it's an extremely simple contract, Mr Vassilis. Just between me and my grandfather—it will have no impact on your own contract with him, I promise. My grandfather undertakes to make a certain amount of money over to me upon my marriage to you.' She smiled again, bright and hard. 'Unlike you, I prefer Coustakis cash, not shares.'

Nikos's face had frozen.

'He is *paying* you to marry me?'

Andrea could have laughed. Laughed right in his handsome face. He was angry! He actually had the nerve to be angry! God, what a hypocrite! But she couldn't laugh. Her throat felt very tight suddenly, as if there was a cord around her neck. Choking at her. All she could do was give a careless, acknowledging nod and take another mouthful of coffee.

She set her cup down with a click.

'Just as he is paying *you*,' she pointed out, 'to marry *me*.'

'That is different! Completely different!'

Refutation was in every syllable. Andrea busied herself topping up her coffee. She felt very calm now. Extremely calm.

'I don't see why. You would hardly hitch yourself to an unknown woman if there weren't something in it for you, would you? I just happen to come with enough Coustakis shares to make it worth your while.' She replaced the coffee pot and looked straight across the table at the man she was going to marry. For half a million pounds.

'Mr Vassilis, let us be completely up-front about this. You did me the courtesy last night—' she did not trouble to hide the sarcasm in her voice '—of pointing out that our marriage was predicated upon your taking control of Coustakis Industries. You can't do that without a majority shareholding. Even I, with my tiny business brain, know that!'

Nikos looked at her. His grey eyes were like cold slate. 'I am *buying* Coustakis shares! Not in cash, but in paper—exchanging them for Vassilis shares at a hefty premium, I assure you! Your grandfather will do very well out of the deal! I'm undertaking a reverse takeover, whereby the much smaller Vassilis Inc can acquire the much larger Coustakis holding with a minimum of debt purchase or rights issues to fund it.'

She waved her hand impatiently. 'Spare me the technicalitics! Thc salient point, so far as I am concerned, is that my grandfather will not agree to the merger—reverse take-over, acquisition, whatever you call it—unless you marry me. That means you're marrying me to get Coustakis Industries. Owning the majority of Coustakis shares will make you even richer than you are—i.e. you're being *paid* to marry me. End of story.'

Tony would be proud of my cool, clear logic, she thought defiantly.

Every good resolution that Nikos had entertained since brooding on Andrea Coustakis in his boardroom vanished. Every last shred of sympathy. Sympathy for her being kept in ignorance by Old Man Coustakis, sympathy for her having a brute like him for a grandfather—all went totally. He had come to make his peace with her, to start over again, begin his wooing of her as a man should woo his bride...

That hysterical harpy he had seen last night would never come back—there would be no need for her. Instead only the soft, yielding, sensual woman he had held in his arms so tantalisingly would be the bride he took for his wife.

But what did he find now? A woman sitting and talking

about marriage and money in the same breath. A woman with a mind like a cash-box.

Conscience pricked at him, but he pushed it away. No, of course he would not have dreamt of marrying an unknown woman without the chance to take over Coustakis Industries! But dynastic marriages of convenience were commonplace in the world of the very rich—that did not mean they had to be sordid. And since setting eyes on Andrea Coustakis he had known straight away that marriage to her would be anything but a marriage of convenience—it would be a marriage of mutual pleasure…

Andrea sat across the table and studied him dispassionately. He was offended. Offended by her frankness. She no longer wanted to laugh. Nor did her throat feel tight any more. Instead, a sort of dull, hard, unemotional carapace had descended on her, covering every inch of her.

As he looked back at her Nikos felt his gaze hardening. *Theos*, but she was a cool piece. Coustakis blood ran in her veins, no doubt about that!

Revulsion shimmered through him. The woman he had held trembling in his arms last night seemed a thousand miles away, as if she had never been. This was the true Andrea Coustakis now. Like her grandfather—knowing the price of everything, the value of nothing.

And she knew her own price, that was for sure. He smiled grimly. Well, he knew her price too. And he would treat her accordingly.

He got to his feet.

'Well—' his voice was abrupt '—since we now both know where we stand, we can begin.'

She looked up at him, uncertain suddenly.

'Begin what?'

He flashed a smile. It had no humour in it.

'Our official betrothal.'

He reached down and took her hand, drawing her to her feet.

'And, though you might wish to seal such an event with a chequebook, I prefer a more traditional method—'

She had a fraction of a second to read his intent. It was utterly inadequate to allow her to react in time and pull away.

His kiss was deep and sensuous. Slow and possessive.

Very, very possessive.

His mouth moved over hers, lazily, exploringly, tastingly... Making absolutely free with her.

She felt her stomach plummet to the floor, felt adrenaline flood through her veins, felt weakness debilitate her totally.

Felt her hand lift of its own accord and curl around his neck, splaying its fingers into his silky hair. Felt herself moan softly, helplessly, as he played with her mouth.

He let her go, casually unwinding her hand and letting it drop nervelessly to her side. Then he took her chin in his fingers and tilted it up. Her mouth was bee-stung, lips red and swollen. Aroused.

Her eyes were lustrous, wide and staring at him, her lashes thick and lush.

'You are an acquisition, Andrea Coustakis, that I shall very much enjoy making,' he said softly, gazing down at her with gleaming possession in his eyes. His voice dropped, making her heart stop. 'I look forward, very much to our personal merger...'

His meaning made perfectly clear, he stroked her cheek and stood back. Then he glanced at his watch.

'Come—we shall lunch, and show the world that Vassilis Inc has plans for Coustakis Industries.'

He tucked her hand into his arm and led her off.

Andrea went with him helplessly. She hadn't a bone left in her body to resist.

The restaurant was plush and crowded. It was clearly excruciatingly expensive. Andrea didn't have to glance at the menu prices to know that.

As they'd walked in, she stiff and wary, concealing her nervousness at being in such a place, she'd felt every eye upon her. A covert glance around showed her that just about everyone here was male—the place was awash with suits. Very expensive suits. This was a place, she knew immediately, where the most successful businessmen in Athens took their lunch and cut their deals, made their contacts and their money.

The maître d' who advanced upon them at their entrance knew her escort, that was obvious. His manner was oh-so-attentive, oh-so-deferential. Though the place looked packed, he did not seem in the least dismayed by the prospect of having to find a table for his latest arrivals.

Nikos knew he'd sort something. For a start he was too curious about the female at his side not to want to find out more. Athens was a city that liked to gossip, and Nikos had made sure that it liked to gossip about him. Having a reputation as a connoisseur of fine women did him no harm at all in the business world. Men envied him—envied his success, his ability to have a beautiful woman on his arm, envied the fact that, unlike most of them, he did not need his money to keep them there—he could do it on his looks alone.

'Kyrios Vassilis,' smiled the greeter. 'How delightful to have you as our guest today. And your lovely companion, of course…'

His voice trailed away expectantly.

With an acknowledging half-smile, Nikos accommodated him.

'Thespiris Coustakis,' he obliged.

The man's face was a picture. Nikos almost laughed. Then, revealing nothing but the excited gleam in his eyes, the man immediately bowed to Andrea and murmured, in breathless tones, how greatly honoured he was to have her grace his establishment.

'No fuss, if you please,' said Nikos, and began to head for the bar area. 'We'll have a drink until our table is ready.' He caught the man's eye and made his message clear. 'Something as private as you can manage.'

'Of course.' The man bowed again, eyes gleaming even more, and clicked his fingers imperiously for a pair of minions, who were there immediately and then despatched variously at his bidding. Then, bowing yet again, he ostentatiously ushered Nikos and Andrea towards the bar.

'This way, if you please, Thespiris Coustakis,' he said, in a voice that was intentionally louder than before. Andrea could see a couple of men seated nearby, also waiting for their table, look up sharply, subjecting her to penetrating stares. Then one of them promptly got up and moved across to one of the tables in the dining area, bending low to speak into the man's ear. The man looked up abruptly and followed his line of gaze towards Nikos Vassilis and his companion.

As she took her seat—a huge, soft leather chair into which she sank almost completely—she said through clenched teeth, 'What the hell is this circus? Have I got two heads or something?'

Nikos gave a brief laugh, his teeth gleaming wolfishly.

'Oh, the show has begun, Andrea, *agape mou*. The show has most very definitely begun.'

It was not the most comfortable meal Andrea had eaten in her life, but it was certainly the most expensive. Not even dinner last night could match lunch today. For a start they were drinking vintage Krug champagne. Andrea did not even want to think what that must have cost. Then there were black truffles, caviar, exotic seafood she couldn't even identify served in a delicate sauce with exquisitely presented vegetables. As well as the champagne Nikos ordered wine as well, and by the reverence with which it was served—from displaying the label for his approval and the sommelier tasting some in his little silver cup, to Nikos's final approving nod as he sampled first the bouquet and then the wine itself—she could see it must be as expensive as the champagne, if not more so.

She wished desperately, as she ate her way through a lunch that it would have taken her six months to pay for herself, that she could enjoy it more. It seemed dreadful to have such expensive food in front of her and yet feel as if she had to force down every mouthful. Tension knotted in her stomach like rope.

It wasn't just that she could see she was being looked over by every person in the restaurant, from the humblest waiter to the richest patron, it was that she was lunching, in public, with Nikos Vassilis.

Who was making it very, very clear just who he was keeping company.

The Coustakis heiress.

It clearly, she thought, her lips tight, gave him one hell of a kick!

He said as much at one point. Leaning closer, as though to whisper some intimacy to her, he murmured, 'They are all agog, Andrea *mou*—your name has gone round like wildfire and they are desperate to know who you are! Strange as it seems, no one in Athens knew Yiorgos Coustakis had a granddaughter—you have been kept as a card up his sleeve! And now—' satisfaction—the satisfaction of a hunger sated, a long hunger born many years ago in the streets of the city—gleamed in his slate eyes '—they can see exactly how the old man has decided to play you! There isn't a man here who does not realise the significance of your being here with me!'

'Is it public knowledge yet that you will be taking over Coustakis Industries?' Andrea asked. She kept her voice cool and businesslike, though it was an effort to do so. Since he had kissed her with such confident possession, sealing their bargain, it had been an effort to do anything except drown her memory of the recalled sensation of his lips tasting her mouth...

He took a mouthful of wine, clearly savouring it, then set down the glass.

'There have been rumours—there are always rumours. After all, Yiorgos is getting older—something must happen to the company. Up till now no one realised he had any heir at all— let alone a hide-away heiress! But now—well, I think they will draw their own conclusions, do you not, *agape mou*?'

'Don't use endearments to me!' she responded sharply. She didn't like the sound of the liquid syllables in his low, intimate voice.

He raised a mocking eyebrow. 'My dear Andrea, we are to

be married. We must, as I have just told you, put on an appropriate show. And, speaking of marriage, what are your wedding plans? I tell you frankly I would hope above all that they are speedy. But other than that you can have free rein. I assume your mother will fly out for it?'

Andrea's face froze. 'No,' she said shortly.

Kim mustn't even know about the wedding. Andrea would have to get Tony to say she was just staying on here for a few weeks, that was all. The last thing she wanted was Kim finding out just what she was planning to do!

'She dislikes your grandfather so much?' There was an edge in Nikos's voice as he remembered Yiorgos saying that Andrea's mother had had very different views on upbringing from him. Well, given Yiorgos's demonstration of grandfatherly chastisement last night, he could hardly be surprised.

'I don't want to talk about it,' said Andrea tightly.

Nikos's eyes narrowed, studying her closed face. There was something wrong here, he thought suddenly. Her eyes were a little too bright, her soft mouth almost trembling beneath the hardened line of her lips. The memory of her standing on the terrace, talking about her father and her mother's memory of him, came back to him. He cursed himself for an insensitive fool.

'I'm sorry,' he said suddenly. 'Of course she would find it distressing to revisit the place where she was so happy with your father.'

'Yes,' said Andrea, swallowing, 'that's it.'

'Then perhaps a private wedding would be best, *ne*?'

'Definitely,' she agreed. 'And as speedily as it can be arranged.'

She reached for her wine glass. She had drunk more than she had meant to, but her nerves, beneath the unemotional carapace that had descended on her, were shaky, she realised. As she moved forward his hand stayed her wrist, closing around it loosely.

'You are so eager to be my wife, Andrea?'

His voice had lowered again, taking on that intimate timbre

that made her go shivery. Her eyes flew to his. In her wrist, as his thumb rubbed casually along the delicate skin over her veins, a pulse throbbed.

'I meant,' she said, as brusquely as she could, 'that you must be keen to get the merger underway as soon as possible.'

She drew her hand away and picked up her wine glass, drinking deeply.

For a moment Nikos hovered between indignation and amusement. Amusement won out. Mocking amusement. She was responsive to him—he had proved that twice already—and he knew perfectly well that he would dissolve any last resistance to him. Knowing now that she was only interested in marrying him for money, he would take particular pleasure in revealing to her just how sexually vulnerable to him he could make her—when he chose. She would leave their marriage bed in no doubt whatsoever that he could turn her into a willing, purring sexual partner, eager to do in bed whatever he wanted her to...

He frowned. A moment ago he had been feeling sorry for her—mourning, with her mother, her lost father. The girl with the cash-box mentality had been completely absent then.

Now she was back with a vengeance.

'As eager to get on with your merger as I am to get my grandfather to release my capital,' she announced crisply.

The phrase sounded good in her ears. Made it sound the sort of thing that heiresses said—the sort of thing that went down well, with approving nods, in places like this. People were still looking at her, she knew. Word had gone round—the Coustakis heiress was in town.

And she was lunching with Nikos Vassilis.

Marriages or corporate mergers—they were all the same thing to people like these.

There was a sour taste in her throat, despite the wine.

CHAPTER SEVEN

LUNCH seemed endless, and it was well into the afternoon before Andrea could finally escape. And even then she could not escape Nikos.

He had phoned his office on his mobile, cancelling all his appointments. That alone, he knew, would accelerate the rumours. Nikos Vassilis never cancelled appointments—he was assiduous in his pursuit of business and profit.

He smiled down at his bride-to-be, an intimate smile that Andrea knew was for the benefit of the remaining diners, as they took their leave from the restaurant. 'I thought that you might like to go shopping. I'm sure you will wish for a spectacular trousseau!'

'I've got all the clothes I need,' she replied sharply. She didn't want any more clothes—the closets in her room at her grandfather's house were groaning. Today, having made the momentous decision to marry Nikos Vassilis, she had changed into one of the outfits Zoe had shown her—a pair of beautifully cut taupe trousers and a shaped appliquéd top. There were more than enough remaining to see her through to her wedding day.

He gave a disbelieving laugh. 'No woman has all the clothes she needs,' he commented dryly.

'I'm not interested in clothes,' she said carelessly.

He laughed again. 'Then you are unique amongst your sex! Besides...' his voice took on a caressing note '...even if you are not interested in clothes, Andrea, they most definitely are interested in you...'

His eyes worked over her torso, blatantly taking in how the jersey material of her top stretched across her full breasts, outlining their generous swell.

Unconsciously she tugged at the hem of her top, as if that would instantly conceal her figure.

'You only reveal yourself more to me,' he said softly, his breath warm on her throat. Fleetingly he ran the back of his hand down her cheek, making her breath catch. 'I would like to choose some clothes for you, Andrea—please allow me that privilege.'

'I told you I had enough!' She pulled away from him, wishing her heart-rate had not suddenly started to race at his touch.

'Something special,' he went on, as if she hadn't spoken, 'for our wedding night.'

She stilled. Then, with a curious twist to her lips, she nodded.

'If you insist.'

He smiled with satisfaction. 'Oh, but I do, *pethi mou*, I do.'

He took her to an exclusive lingerie boutique in the chic Kolonaki shopping area of Athens. It was the kind of place, Andrea thought, where if you asked for a cotton bra and panties they would throw you out! It was also the kind of place, she realised, the moment the attentive assistant started to fawn all over her escort, where Nikos Vassilis was clearly an extremely valued customer indeed.

And it didn't take a genius for Andrea to guess just what kind of woman he bought lingerie here for!

Oh, the assistant was polite enough to her, that was for sure, but it was obvious that she regarded her actual customer as Nikos Vassilis. Andrea knew she had been labelled a passing floozy with a single glance! She let the woman take her measurements and whisk out one gauzy confection after another, but declined the offer to try anything on.

She wouldn't be wearing any of it anyway. Her wedding night would be short—and very far from sweet.

Well satisfied with his purchases, Nikos was all set to keep going.

'Come,' he said persuasively, 'we are surrounded by designer shops—take your pick!'

'No, thanks,' she returned indifferently. 'I keep telling you I've got enough.'

'Then do me one favour, *ne*?' He caught her arm. 'Let me buy you a single skirt, now, to change into. You have worn trousers two days running. I far prefer women to wear skirts.'

'How surprising,' she said with a wry smile. 'Unfortunately for you, I don't wear skirts.'

He frowned. 'What do you mean, you don't wear skirts?'

'Exactly that,' she replied.

'You wore an evening dress last night!'

'That was long,' she said briefly. She wanted to change the subject—fast.

Enlightenment dawned on him—and relief. For a moment he had feared that she was the type of female who made some kind of nonsensical stand about insisting on wearing trousers on principle. Nikos saw no sense in such an attitude. He was no chauvinist—Vassilis Inc was unusual, he knew, in taking a proactive stance on hiring and promoting women—but he saw no reason why a woman should think she became demeaned as a sex object just for wearing a skirt!

Now he realised this was not Andrea's attitude.

'I'm sure your legs are beautiful,' he reassured her. 'They are long and elegant and shapely—I can see that even now.'

She glanced up at him. The curious twist was on her mouth again.

'Can you? You must have X-ray vision.'

He smiled indulgently. 'Even if they are not your best point, *agape mou*, I can make allowances.'

The twist to her mouth deepened, but she said nothing.

'So,' he said, 'let us buy you a skirt—and I will set your fears at rest.'

Her face went blank.

'I've done enough shopping for today. I'm bored.'

His eyebrow rose. He knew of no woman who was bored by shopping—especially when it was his money they were spending. Esme, naturally, was obsessed by clothes and her own appearance—it was her profession, after all. And Xanthe adored being taken by him to her favourite jewellers' shops. She was like a magpie for jewellery, and decked herself in glitter whenever she could. For her, Nikos knew with a cynical tightening of his jaw, it was an insurance policy for her old age, when she could no longer hold her rich lovers to her side.

Perhaps Andrea, born to expectations of vast wealth from birth, saw things in a different light.

'Well, I would hate you to be bored, so how can I amuse you?'

Andrea didn't like the note in his voice, hinting at meanings she would rather ignore. Didn't like it at all. She started walking along the pavement.

'I want to go sightseeing,' she said suddenly. After all, she would never come to Athens again. She might as well go sightseeing now, while she could.

A pang hit her, hard and painful. This was her father's city. He had been raised here. His blood sang in her veins. She was as Greek as she was English—and this was the first time in her life she was setting foot on Greek soil. And the last.

Sadness swept through her—sadness and bitterness.

'Sightseeing?' Nikos queried. 'But you will have seen all the sights a hundred times!'

She stared at him. 'I've never been to Athens before—never been to Greece before.'

Nikos looked at her, disapproval in his expression. It was one thing for Andrea's English mother to be worried about her father-in-law's views on disciplining children, or unwilling to revisit her dead husband's country herself, quite another to forbid her daughter to visit at all. It was bad enough Andrea did not speak Greek, let alone that she had never been here! He'd assumed that although Yiorgos Coustakis had not paraded his granddaughter to the world, she had, of course, been out here for holidays and so forth

'Then it is high time,' he said decisively, 'that I show you Athens.'

And he did. They spent the afternoon doing what all first-time tourists in the city did—climbing the Acropolis to pay homage to the glory of the first flowering of Western civilisation, the Parthenon.

Andrea was enthralled, refusing to acknowledge the wave of desolation that swept over her at the thought that soon, all too soon, she would never see Nikos again.

It didn't matter how much her eyes were drawn to him; it didn't matter how much she revelled in drinking in, as secretly as she could, the bounty that was this paean to manhood at her side. All of this, heady and intoxicating as she increasingly found his company, was nothing more than a temporary interlude in her life. Nikos Vassilis, though he could send a shiver of electricity through her with a single glance, the barest brush of his sleeve on her arm, was nothing more than a temporary interlude.

It was a phrase Andrea forced herself to remember day after day as, for the next two weeks, Nikos Vassilis made it very clear to the rest of the world that he had snapped up the Coustakis heiress as his forthcoming bride and that his sights were set, very firmly, on Coustakis Industries.

Andrea wished she could get used to him squiring her around—lunching in fashionable restaurants, dining in fashionable nightspots, always at her side, attentive, possessive, ramming home to all who saw them, time after time, that he was the favoured choice of Yiorgos Coustakis for the rich prize of Coustakis Industries—but she could not. Every time he picked her up in his gleaming, purring, powerful Ferrari she felt a kick go through her like an electric shock.

She did her best to hide it. Did her best to maintain the stony façade that she knew, instinctively, annoyed him.

Almost as much as it amused him.

'My English ice-maiden,' he said to her softly one evening, as she deliberately turned her face away from his greeting so that his lips could only brush her cheek, 'how I will enjoy melting you.'

She might think she was only marrying him to extract her

capital from the covetous claws of Old Man Coustakis—but he would prove otherwise.

And take great relish in it!

'You're mussing my hair, Nikos,' she replied snappily.

'It will get a lot more mussed than that soon,' he replied, eyes gleaming with mocking amusement—and promise. 'Tonight,' he went on, 'we shall go dancing.' He leant forward. 'I long to hold you in my arms again, Andrea *mou*.'

She backed away, almost tripping.

'I don't dance,' she said abruptly.

He laughed. The sound of it made her feel irritated. Among other things she didn't want to put a name to.

With every passing day her feet were getting colder and colder. She would wake in the middle of the night and the sheer disbelief of what she was doing would wash over and over her. Only one thought kept her going—money. Money at last. She had to hold out—hold out until the money was in the bank.

Then she could cut and run—and run and run...

From demons she refused to give a name to.

'I wasn't suggesting we go hot-clubbing till dawn,' he assured her. 'Since it isn't your scene anyway, I recall, I was thinking of something a little more....sophisticated. I think you will enjoy it. I know I will...'

She compressed her mouth. 'I said I don't dance. I mean it.'

He smiled lazily down at her, his mockery at her refusal glittering in his eyes like gold glinting in a sheet of slate, 'I can see I shall have to persuade you otherwise.'

He let the tips of his fingers brush lightly along her arm, amused at the way she jerked away again. He knew just how to handle her now, baiting her with her own responsiveness to him. She didn't like being that responsive, she was fighting against it, but it would be a losing battle, he knew.

And the victory would be his.

A sweet victory—reduced to abject pleading for his lovemaking this woman who made it totally, shamelessly clear that the only reason she was marrying him was to gain control of the capital her grandfather held for her. That would be a victory he would savour to the full.

As for Andrea, all she could do was put her mask in place and try and get through the evening.

Despite her protestations Nikos took her out later that night, and though it was not some packed and heaving strobe-lit club, there was no way she was going to let him lead her out onto the small, intimate floor in the rooftop restaurant he took her to.

'I said I don't dance and I meant it!' she repeated.

'Try,' he said. There was a glint in his eye, and it was not entirely predatory. There was determination in it as well.

Andrea gave in.

He led her out—she as stiff as a board—onto the dance floor. A love song was playing, and though with one part of her mind she was grateful, with the rest of it she felt her terror only increased, for reasons which had nothing to do with her habitual refusal to dance.

Nikos slid his arms around her, resting on the curve of her hips at either side. They burned through the thin fabric of her long peacock-blue dress with a warmth that made the pulse in her neck beat faster. She stood immobile. Her legs began to ache with the tension.

'Put your arms around my neck, *pethi mou*.'

The warmth of his breath on her ear made her shiver. He was too close. Much, much too close. The long, lean line of his body pressed against her, hip to hip, thigh to thigh.

Don't think! Don't feel! she adjured herself desperately.

Gingerly, very gingerly, she lifted her arms and placed one palm on either shoulder.

He was in evening dress, and the dark fabric felt smooth and rich to the touch. Beneath the jacket she could feel the hardness of his shoulders. She tensed even more.

'Relax,' he murmured, and with the slightest of pressures on her hip started to move her around with him.

For a brief moment she went with him, her right foot moving

jerkily in the direction he was urging her. Her legs were like wood, unbending.

'Relax,' he said again.

She moved her left leg, catching up with him, and they repeated the movement—him smoothly, she with a jerkiness that she could not control. Her spine was beginning to hurt with the effort.

She lasted another ten seconds, her face rigid, willing herself to keep going. Then, with a little cry, she stumbled away from him.

'I can't! I can't do this!'

She broke across the little dance floor, desperate to sit down, and collapsed back on her chair. Nikos was there in an instant beside her.

'What the hell was that about?' he demanded.

She could hear the annoyance in his voice. Only the annoyance.

'I told you, I don't dance!' she bit at him.

'Don't? Or won't?' he asked thinly, and sat down himself. He seized at the neck of the champagne bottle nestling in its ice bucket and refilled his glass. Hers was almost untouched.

'When we are married,' he said, setting down his glass with a snap, 'I shall give you lessons.'

'You do that,' she replied, and took a gulp of her champagne.

Nikos Vassilis would never teach her to dance.

Or anything else.

Surreptitiously, under the table, she slowly rubbed at her thighs. The ache went right through to her bones. And beyond.

Andrea clenched the phone to her ear.

'You're sure? You're absolutely sure?'

'Yes, Miss Fraser, completely sure. The sum of five hundred thousand pounds has been credited to your account.'

'And it can't be removed without my permission?' Her question was sharp.

'Certainly not!' The voice of the bank official, a thousand miles away in London, sounded deeply shocked as he replied.

It was the morning of Andrea's wedding.

The happiest day of my life! The day I finally, finally wave a wand over Mum and start our new lives!

As she terminated the call, with repeated assurances from her bank that the money deposited in her account first thing that day was totally and irrevocably hers to dispose of as she would, deep, deep relief flooded through her. She had done it! She had got what she had come for—the promise of freedom from poverty, from ill-health, from the grind and drab penury her mother had put up with for twenty-five years.

Now all she had to do was endure the next twenty-four hours and she would be on her way home.

I can do it! I've done it so far and I can do this last thing!

'*Kyria*, may I start to dress you, please?' Zoe's voice sounded anxiously from the doorway. 'Kyrios Coustakis would like you to go downstairs as soon as possible.'

Andrea nodded, and the lengthy process of dressing Yiorgos Coustakis's illegitimate granddaughter for her wedding to the man who would run his company and give him the heir he craved got underway.

Andrea felt the relief drain out of her, replaced by a tightness that started to wind around her lungs like biting cord. As she sat in front of the looking glass, Zoe skilfully pinning up her hair, she stared at her reflection. Her eyes seemed too big, her skin too pale. She clenched her hands together in her lap. The reality of what she was about to do hit her, over and over again, like repeated blows.

For all that it was a small, private wedding, it seemed to go on for ever, Andrea thought bleakly. She stood beside her bridegroom, unsmiling, her throat so tight she could hardly say the words that bound her to the tall, straight figure at her side. Sickness churned in her stomach.

She was marrying him! She was actually marrying Nikos Vassilis. Here. Now. Right now. Faintness drummed at her.

Her legs and spine ached with the tension wiring her whole body taut.

There was a ring on her finger. She could see it glinting in the sunlight.

It doesn't mean anything! This time tomorrow he'll have packed me off back to London and wished me good riddance. He'll have what he wanted—my grandfather's company. He'll be glad to see the back of me. He never wanted me in the first place.

And he doesn't even intend to be faithful…

Her lips compressed. Three nights ago her grandfather had summoned her again. Nikos had returned her from yet another night out, this time a concert, where the combination of Dvorak and Rachmaninov, plus the thrill of hearing one of the world's greatest soloists give the Dvorak cello concerto, had conspired to weaken her façade. As they left the concert hall she had turned impulsively to Nikos.

'That was wonderful! Thank you!'

Her eyes were shining, her face radiant.

Nikos paused and looked down at her. 'I'm glad to have given you pleasure.'

For once there was no double meaning in his words, no sensual glint in his eyes. For a moment they just looked at each other. Andrea's ears rang with the echo of the tumultuous finale of the Rachmaninov symphony. Her heart was almost as tumultuous.

Her eyes entwined with his and something flowed between them. She could not tell what it was, but it was something that made her want the moment to last for ever.

She was almost regretful that in fact she never was going to be his wife in anything but briefest name.

It was a regret that had been destroyed in the two-minute conversation with her grandfather on her return to his villa.

'There are things to make clear to you,' he began in his harsh, condemning voice, as she stood unspeaking in front of him to receive her lecture. 'From the moment you become Nikos Vassilis's wife you will behave as a Greek wife should.

He will teach you the obedience you so sorely lack!' His soul-less eyes rested on her like a basilisk, 'You will understand that you will gain no privileges from your connection with me. Nor should you imagine that you will gain any privileges from the fact that you are handsome enough for your husband to find you, for the moment, sexually desirable.'

He saw the expression on her face and gave a short laugh. 'I said "for the moment" and that is what I meant! Understand this, girl—' his eyes bored into hers '—in Greece a man who is a husband is still a man. And his wife must know her place. Which is to be *silent*! Nikos Vassilis has two mistresses cur-rently—an American model, a tramp who sleeps with any man who passes, and a woman of Athens who is a professional whore. He will discard neither for your sake.' His voice dropped menacingly. 'If I hear any whining from you, any screeching tantrums because of this, you will regret it! Do you understand?'

She understood all right and she felt revulsion shimmer through her.

Be grateful you're not marrying him for real!

But marrying him she was—if she wanted money for Kim then she must go through this farce of a wedding ceremony.

Not one mistress but two! Her mouth twisted. My, my, what a busy lad Nikos Vassilis was! And still intended to be, so it seemed! Well, that might be the way Greek males saw the world, but she would be having none of it!

The pop of a champagne bottle made her jump, exacerbating her jittery nerves. One of the servants was pouring out foaming liquid into tall glasses. Andrea sipped at hers and looked around her.

All this money, all this wealth, all this opulence and luxury, she thought. I've been drowning in it for two weeks, nearly three.

I want to go home!

The thought caught at her, making her want to cry out with it. She wanted to go home, back to Kim, back to the poky, damp flat that Nikos Vassilis would be appalled to know she had grown up in! He thought he was marrying the Coustakis heiress. What a joke! What a ludicrous, ridiculous joke!

Well, the joke would be on him before the night was out.

But she didn't feel like laughing.

Andrea sat in the Louis Quinze armchair, her eyes shut. The champagne had been drunk, she had endured the painfully polite congratulations of the household staff, and now she was waiting for her brand-new husband to emerge out of the library, where her grandfather was finally allowing him to sign the merger contracts. A bevy of men in suits had arrived on the doorstep an hour ago, all with aides and briefcases, and disappeared into the inner sanctum of Yiorgos Coustakis to conduct the real business of the day.

Her legs ached. Carefully she rubbed them through the material of her trousers. Zoe had helped her change out of the long ivory satin gown she had worn for the ceremony, and now she was back in the clothes she had arrived in. Although the staff had emptied just about the whole of the closet into half a dozen suitcases to see her through her honeymoon, Andrea had insisted on her own small case—the one she had brought with her—being handed to her personally. She had packed it the night before, with all her own clothes and the make-up bag containing the key to the airport locker holding her money and passport, right after phoning Tony and telling him that she was coming home in forty-eight hours, and asking him, as always, to give her love to Kim. She hadn't spoken to her mother since arriving here. Hadn't been able to bring herself to. She knew Kim would understand, would make do with having her love passed on every day by Tony.

The ormolu clock on the gilded mantelpiece ticked quietly. The room was silent. The only sound in it was Andrea's heavy heartbeat.

Let me just get through tonight, and then I can be gone!

There was the click of a door opening across the marbled hall, and the sound of voices. She opened her eyes. She could hear the besuited visitors taking their leave, their business done.

Time for Nikos to move on to the next item on his agenda—taking his bride on honeymoon, thought Andrea viciously. Being angry seemed like a good idea right now.

Safer.

She heard Nikos's voice in the hallway, and her grandfather answering shortly. Then footsteps as her grandfather trod heavily back to his own affairs. It must have been a good day's work for him, Andrea thought, selling his company and his bastard granddaughter at the same time.

Something flickered in the corner of her eye, and she twisted her head. It was just a drape, fluttering in the breeze from the open window. The day was warm, the sun inviting. Something caught at her heart, an echo from very long ago, from long before she was born.

Out of nowhere a memory came. A memory of something that had never happened but that she had so often, as a child, wished so ardently were real, and not a mere hopeless longing. The memory of her father, kind and smiling, calling her his princess, her mother his queen, crowning them both with happiness...

But it had never happened. Never. Instead he had died before she was born.

It shouldn't have been like this!

The silent cry came from deep inside her.

But it *is* like this, and there's nothing more I can do about it than I have already done.

'Are you ready?'

Nikos's voice was harsh, cutting through her sombre thoughts. He sounded tense.

She got to her feet.

'Yes,' she answered, and walked towards him where he stood in the doorway.

They took their places in the back of her grandfather's vast limousine, Andrea sinking back so far into the seat that she felt she would disappear. Nikos threw himself into the other corner. The car moved forward smoothly.

They did not talk, and Andrea was glad. She had nothing to

say to this man now. After tomorrow morning she would never see him again. He was a passing stranger, nothing more.

'Would you like a drink?'

She blinked. Nikos was pulling out a concealed drinks compartment, revealing an array of crystal decanters. She shook her head. He lifted one of the decanters and poured a measure of its contents into a glass. Andrea could smell whisky. He knocked it back in one shot, then replaced the glass and slid shut the cabinet.

'How are you feeling?'

The abrupt question took her by surprise. She shrugged.

'OK,' she said indifferently.

He made a sound in his throat that sounded to her ears like an impatient sigh, and then, with a swift movement, he loosened the tie at his throat and undid his collar. Andrea couldn't help looking across at him.

Immediately she wished he hadn't. She didn't know what it was about loosened ties and opened shirt collars, but the kick to her guts was immediate. Nikos ran a hand roughly through his hair, ruffling its satin smoothness. Another kick went straight through her guts.

To her relief, he wasn't paying her any attention, simply staring moodily out through the smoked glass window. Then, abruptly, he spoke.

'*Theos*, but I'm glad that's over!'

The kick in Andrea's guts vanished instantly. He was glad it was over. Fine. So was she. Very glad. Very glad indeed. Couldn't have been gladder. Her lips pressed together.

She looked away, staring out of her own window, and heard Nikos shift in his seat.

'Don't sulk, Andrea,' he told her tersely. 'You enjoyed that ordeal as little as I did! But it's over now. Thank God!' Then, on an even terser note, he said, 'Did you get your money?'

There was condemnation in his voice. Andrea thought of the merger contracts, signed not half an hour ago. Making Nikos Vassilis one of the richest men in Europe.

'Of course,' she answered.

'You won't need it,' said the man she had married. 'I will give you everything you want.'

She didn't reply.

He gave another, heavier sigh.

'Andrea, this is a time for plain speaking. We are married. And there is absolutely no reason to suppose things will not work out between us! Your grandfather is out of the picture now. He does not concern us. It is up to us to make this marriage work, and I believe it can—very successfully. If we both just make an effort to make it work! I am prepared to do so—and I ask that you are too. As soon as our honeymoon is over we shall fly to England to meet your mother, and mend bridges there. However much she disapproved of your grandfather, I hope she will think more kindly of me.'

She'll never lay eyes on you, thought Andrea, never even know you exist.

Nikos was talking still.

'For now you must put your mind to where we shall live. For the moment I propose my apartment in Athens, but I would prefer, I admit, a more permanent property. We can have a house in London, of course, for when you want to be with your English relatives, and I suggest we buy a villa on one of the islands as well, where we can relax in private.'

'Fine,' said Andrea. The issue was academic; it didn't matter what she said.

Tonight, she thought, over dinner, or perhaps, better still, in the hotel suite, where I don't have to worry about waiters hovering or other diners looking us over, I can tell him the truth about me. That will put an end to this farce.

Nikos gave up. He had done his best to be civil, but enough was enough. He felt rough. He had been working like crazy ever since Old Man Coustakis had dangled the prospect of a takeover in front of him. Mergers and acquisitions didn't happen overnight—the planning and preparation involved was immense. On top of that he still had to keep Vassilis Inc rolling along, even while he was gearing it up to ingest the much larger Coustakis Industries. It had not, he thought grimly, been the best time to have to go off wooing a bride! Nevertheless he had found the time to squire Andrea around, knowing that being seen prominently in public with her was all part of convincing the Athens business community—and beyond—of the reality of his intentions towards Coustakis Industries.

But for all the evenings spent taking Andrea out he was still no closer to seeing anything more of her than the closed, controlled surface she presented to him. There was certainly a deal of English blood in her, all right, he thought, exasperated. All that cool, calm, collected front she insisted on—polite, but distant. The only time he'd seen any trace of enthusiasm in her had been the other evening at the concert—then her eyes had shone like glossy chestnuts in autumn, and a vitality had filled her usually deadpan expression, catching at him. For a moment, he recalled, as he had looked down at her something had moved in her eyes....

But that had been the only moment. Maybe he had just imagined it anyway. Certainly the only way he was guaranteed to get a reaction from her was by reminding her, as he took such satisfaction in doing, of just how fragile that English sang-froid of hers really was! Of how a single touch could set her thrumming with sexual awareness of him. *That* was the only currency she responded to! However much she tried to suppress her responsiveness to him.

He looked across at her. She was still staring out of the window, ignoring him. Well, let her! It gave him the opportunity to look her over. Catalogue, in his discerning mind, all her sensual charms—from the generous fullness of her mouth to the richness of her breasts, the long line of her legs...

He felt himself relax for the first time that day. It was done. Today had set the seal on his long, long ascent from the rough streets of Athens to the pinnacle of his achievements.

And he knew exactly how to celebrate.

He closed his eyes and gave himself to the pleasure of contemplating just how good it would be to have the woman beside him beneath him.

* * *

'Where the hell are we?'

Andrea's voice was sharp.

'Piraeus,' replied Nikos. 'The port of Athens.'

'The *what*?'

'The port of Athens,' Nikos repeated. 'Where we embark.'

'*Embark?*'

Nikos looked across at her. Now what was she making a fuss about?

Andrea gazed wildly out of the window. She had been paying no attention to their journey from her grandfather's villa, deliberately diverting her mind from what she had just done by thinking about what would be involved in moving Kim out to Spain as soon as possible. But instead of drawing up outside some five-star hotel in the middle of Athens, whence she could easily take a taxi to the airport the following morning, the car had stopped on what she could now see was a quayside, alongside what seemed to be a huge, gleaming vessel.

The chauffeur opened her door and stood back to let her get out. Stiffly, aware that her legs had suddenly started to ache again with unexpected tension, Andrea climbed out and looked around her.

There was a vessel moored at the quayside all right. Absolutely huge. Vast. Stretching like a gleaming monster from bow to stern. A wide gangplank faced her.

'Come,' said Nikos.

He took her arm.

'I'm not going aboard that! What the hell is it?'

His mouth tightened. Hadn't Yiorgos even bothered to tell his granddaughter about his latest spending spree?

'It's your grandfather's new toy,' he told her. 'He's lent it to us for our honeymoon.'

Andrea stared. 'I thought we were going to spend the night in Athens. At a hotel.'

'What for?' countered Nikos. 'We might as well set sail as soon as possible.'

'I'm not going on that thing!'

Her face was set. Aware, as she was blissfully not, of the

highly interested if superficially indifferent attention not only of the chauffeur but of the crewmen at the foot of the gangplank, Nikos impelled her forward. He was not about to have his brand-new bride balk him.

She stumbled slightly, and with a sudden gesture Nikos swept her up into his arms. She gave a small shriek, but Nikos only gave a victor's laugh.

'I'm carrying you over the threshold.' He grinned down at her, as much for the sake of his audience as himself, and plunged up the gangplank.

Short of screaming blue murder, Andrea had no option but to let herself be carried aboard the monstrous vessel. She was too terrified to struggle in case they both landed in the murky water lapping beneath the gangplank.

Nikos set her down on the deck and said something in Greek to the man standing there. Hurriedly she smoothed down her jacket and tried to regain her composure. Then Nikos was introducing her.

'This is Captain Petrachos, Andrea *mou*,' he said smoothly.

Andrea took in a smartly dressed middle-aged man in an immaculate white naval uniform, with a lot of rings around his cuffs and gold epaulettes, sporting a trim, nautical beard.

'Welcome aboard, Kyria Vassilis. I hope you have a very enjoyable voyage.'

'Thank you,' she murmured in a strangled voice. It wouldn't be an enjoyable voyage, she thought wildly, it would be a very short one!

'If you're both ready, I'll get her underway.'

'Thank you,' said Nikos. He held out a hand to Andrea. 'Come, let us explore.'

His fingers closed around hers, tighter than was strictly necessary. Meekly, Andrea went off with him. She was rearranging her thoughts as quickly as possible. OK, so she had assumed— rashly so, it seemed!—that they would spend the first night of their honeymoon at some luxury hotel in the middle of Athens. Instead they were launching out on this floating private liner! Well, she thought grimly, so what? Her ludicrous marriage could come to a speedy and ignominious end here as well as anywhere else! They'd be docked right back here again before tomorrow morning.

Despite her best intentions to remain indifferent to her oh-so-temporary accommodation, Andrea found her eyes widening automatically as Nikos conducted her around the boat.

It was opulent beyond belief! Everywhere she looked there was rare wood panelling, silk, velvet and leather upholstery, gold and silver fittings, cashmere, suede and skins on floors and walls, inlays and gilding all around. A fortune must have been paid to fit out the interior, let alone the cost of the massive yacht itself, thought Andrea.

As they were shown round by an oh-so-attentive chief steward, Andrea felt increasingly oppressed. What had Nikos called it? Her grandfather's latest toy...

On the upper deck, she watched the mainland of Greece slip away behind them as the yacht nosed out towards the open sea. Meanwhile Nikos watched the wind billow through Andrea's exquisite hair. Her face was set. Clearly she was still in a mood.

Nikos's expression hardened. Just how spoilt was this woman? he thought. Here she was, aboard a yacht that was the last word in extravagance, and she still wasn't happy! He thought back to the days of his childhood, so long ago, when he had been a no-hope street kid. No pampered upbringing for him! He had got here, to the deck of a luxury yacht, as head of one of Europe's largest companies, Coustakis Industries, by his own efforts.

And now he was married to Yiorgos Coustakis's grand-daughter.

Well, he had better make the most of it...

CHAPTER EIGHT

CHAMPAGNE beaded in Andrea's glass, fizzing gently. She took another sip. Across the table from her, Nikos did likewise. They were in the dining room—a vast expanse dominated by a huge ebony table, lavishly set with crystal and gold. A suffocating smell of lilies permeated the atmosphere, emanating from the banks of bouquets all around the room. Above their heads a vast chandelier shed its light upon them. Four uniformed stewards stood in a line to one side, ready to do the slightest thing that the honeymoon couple required of them. Deep below the steady thrum of the vessel's motor was the only indication that they were actually on board a boat—the windows were obliterated by vast swathes of black velvet, tasselled in gold, reflecting the gold and black patterning in the deep, soft carpet under Andrea's feet.

She picked at her food. It had probably cost a fortune, just like everything else around her.

'You would prefer something else?' Nikos broke the oppressive silence.

'No, thank you. I'm simply not hungry.' Andrea's voice sounded more clipped than she intended, but civility was hard to project right now. Her whole body felt as if it had been tied into an excruciatingly tight knot.

You've got to tell him! End this farce right now! Then you can go to bed—alone!—and the yacht can start heading back to port.

She wished she had managed to talk to Nikos earlier. She should have stopped him leaving her alone on the deck, when he, with nothing more than a brief, 'There are a few matters I must attend to—excuse me,' disappeared into the interior. But he had not reappeared until a short while ago. In the meantime a stewardess had politely enquired when she would like dinner served, and when she would like to change for it. Helplessly, Andrea had gone along with her, telling her to refer to Mr Vassilis re the timing of dinner.

My, what a good little Greek wife I sound! she had thought. *Deferring to my husband right from the start!*

Husband—the word echoed in her brain.

I'm in shock, she thought, as her fork lifted mechanically to her mouth. I never really believed this would happen. I blanked it out, focussed only on the money for Kim. But it's real; it happened. I married Nikos Vassilis today and he's sitting opposite me, and I *still* haven't told him that this is going to be the shortest marriage in history!

So tell him now!

I should send away the crew, she thought—get rid of them all. Then simply open my mouth and tell him I'm leaving in the morning.

Instead, she found her mind wandering off. What on earth did all those stewards think? she wondered. A pair of newly-weds eating in stony silence? Did they think anything? Did they care? Were they even human? Their faces were totally expressionless. She had a sudden vision of them being androids, like something out of science fiction, and had to suppress a hysterical laugh. Quickly she snapped her mind onto something else.

Like who on earth had been in charge of the interior design of this place? They should be taken out and shot, she thought viciously. To spend such money for such atrocious results seemed like a criminal offence. The décor was hideous, just hideous!

Nikos looked across at her. Her eyes were working around the room disdainfully. Was she picking out flaws, signs of cheapness? he wondered sourly. He glanced down at her plate. She had stopped eating.

With sudden decision Nikos pushed his plate away from him. He was in no mood to eat. No mood to go on sitting here,

with a row of statues like a silent Greek chorus witnessing his
bride display her feelings about marrying him.

He got to his feet. Andrea started, and looked up at him.

'Come.'

He held out a hand to her. His mouth was a thin line.

She hesitated a fraction. There was something about him that
unnerved her, but at the same time she, too, felt an overpowering urge to get out of this oppressive room. And after all she
needed to speak privately with him, so she might as well go
with him.

As he headed towards the door one of the stewards was there
before him, attentively opening it. Andrea hurried after Nikos
in the same tight green evening dress she'd worn her first night
in Greece as he strode along the wide, thickly carpeted corridor.
He flung open a door at the end and held it for her.

She went inside.

It was their bedroom.

Mahogany panelled the room from floor to ceiling, and in
the middle a gigantic bed, swathed in gold silk, held centre
stage. Ornate gold light fittings marched around the room. She
dragged her eyes away.

Do it—do it now!

'I've got something to tell you.'

Andrea's voice sounded high-pitched and clipped.

'How remarkable. My silent bride deigns to speak.'

His sarcasm cut at her. She lifted her chin.

'You might as well know,' she said, 'I'm going back to
England tomorrow. I'm filing for divorce.'

Nikos stared at her, completely stilled. The grey of his eyes
was like cold, hard slate. Andrea felt her hands clench at her
sides. Her legs had started to ache, sensing the tension in the
rest of her body.

'You are mistaken.'

The brief, bald sentence was quietly spoken, but the nape of
Andrea's neck crawled.

'I'm not staying with you!' The pitch of her voice had risen.

'And may I be permitted to ask—' the icy softness cut slivers of flesh from her '—what has led you to make this…un-expected announcement?'

Somehow she managed to stand her ground.

'I should have thought it was obvious! Your sole purpose in marrying me was to clear the way to get hold of my grandfather's company. Now you've done that you don't need to stay married to me for a second longer!'

'An interesting analysis, but fatally flawed,' he returned.

'Why?' she demanded.

'Because,' said Nikos in that same soft voice which now, instead of cutting slivers from her, had somehow, she did not know how, started to send shivers of a quite different nature quivering down her arms, 'you happen to possess charms beyond your possession of Yiorgos Coustakis's DNA. Charms,' he went on—and now the shivers spread from her arms across her breasts, her flanks, 'that I fully intend to enjoy.'

He took a step towards her, the expression in his eyes making it totally, absolutely clear just what charms he had in mind.

She jerked backwards.

'Stay away!'

He stopped again. 'Don't give me orders, *pethi mou*. You'll find I don't respond well to them!'

The edge in his voice, steel beneath the velvet, was a warning.

It was also a trip point.

'If you're after sex go and phone for one of your mistresses!' she flung at him.

He stopped dead.

'My what?'

'You heard me—your mistresses! You're running two that the whole world knows about and God knows how many more besides! Go and phone for one of them if you're feeling horny. But don't damn well come near me!'

His eyes were like splinters.

'And just how, may I ask, did you come by this information?'

'Oh, I got a full briefing from my grandfather! It was part

of his pre-wedding lecture to me not to kick up a fuss about you still having sex with other women. An obedient Greek wife—' she let the sarcasm flow into her voice '—doesn't make a scene over such trifles as her husband's mistresses!'

Comprehension flooded Nikos's expression, masked by anger. Not at Andrea, but at her wretched grandfather. So that was why the girl had done nothing but sulk all day! Thanks, Yiorgos, for another big favour you've done me! Screwing up my marriage before I even get started on it!

'Right,' he began, 'we'll get a few things clear, I think. Firstly, yes, of course I have had liaisons with other women— I was free to do so and I did! But—' he held up his hand '—I have not set eyes on another woman since the day I met you.'

His assurance left Andrea less than impressed.

'So you just dumped them, did you? Charming!'

Nikos shut his eyes briefly, then opened them. 'My relationships with both women are—were—what you might call "open",' he said. 'Xanthe Palloupis has several other rich lovers who help keep her in the style she fully intends to hold on to for as long as her looks last, and Esme Vandersee—'

'Esme Vandersee? The supermodel?' Andrea's voice cut in incredulously. 'She's one of the world's most beautiful women!'

There was a note in her voice that Nikos did not miss, and it sent a shaft of satisfaction through him which, right now, he badly needed. It had been something between dismay and jealousy.

'She is also,' he said, 'quite happy to reward a large assortment of her chosen admirers with a hands-on tour of her spectacular body. I'm confident she found it extremely easy to replace me,' he finished dryly.

But Andrea didn't want to hear about Esme Vandersee and her spectacular body. In fact if the supermodel had suddenly beamed aboard right in front of her she would have got a dusty reception from her lover's bride. Extremely dusty.

She quelled the stab of pure possessiveness that darted through her at the thought of Esme Vandersee or Xanthe

Whatever-her-name-was making moves on Nikos Vassilis. It was utterly inappropriate.

And totally irrelevant.

Why am I discussing Nikos's mistresses? she thought. They've got nothing to do with why I'm going home tomorrow!

'So,' Nikos continued smoothly, 'now I understand the reason for your ill-temper all day, Andrea *mou*—'

'I'm still leaving tomorrow morning! And it's got nothing to do with any of the women you put out for! I have absolutely no intention of staying married to you!'

The glitter was back in Nikos's eyes.

'And what objection, may I ask again, are you going to put forward now?'

Her eyes flicked to the opulence all around them. Kim's entire flat would just about fit into the space of this single stateroom! *Tell him the truth about yourself now—he'll send you packing the moment he hears!*

'For heaven's sake, how could I possibly even *think* of being married to you? We come from totally different worlds—'

She broke off. Something was in his face that made her feel frightened suddenly.

Different world? Oh, yes, different worlds indeed. A fatherless street boy and a pampered heiress...

'Nevertheless...' the softness was back in his voice, and it was slicing at her flesh again '...you are my wife, Andrea Vassilis, and if you understand nothing about what it means to be Greek, understand this—no husband lets his bride make a laughing stock of him by walking out on him straight after their wedding! And never, ever—' his eyes slid over her face, her body '—before their wedding night...'

He came towards her. She could not move. Slate eyes fixed her where she was. Slate eyes with only one purpose in them.

The fear dissolved. For a brief moment desire flooded through her, powerful and irresistible. She crushed it aside. There was no place for it. There could not be. There must not be. In its place came a flat, dull resolve. So it was going to be

like this, was it? Very well, so be it. She'd see it through to
the bitter end—and be on a plane home tomorrow.

She stood there motionless. In her mind she searched for the
impenetrable mask she had donned every time she was in his
company. It was time to wear it again.

He stopped in front of her. She was very still. Like a statue.
He reached a hand towards her. The back of his fingers brushed
her cheek, trailing down over the column of her neck, turning
to close over the cusp of her shoulder, bared except for the
narrow straps of her dress.

'The last time you wore this you melted into my arms like
honey on a warm spoon.'

The thumb of his other hand came up to ease along the
trembling line of her lips.

She stiffened, clutching the carapace to her.

She was holding out on him. Denying her response to him.
He smiled. This and this alone was the way to communicate
with the woman who today had been joined in matrimony to
him. And when, eventually, she lay beneath him, and throbbed
in his embrace, then—oh, then—let her think of the 'different
worlds' they came from. Let her think of the 'release of capital'
she'd gained today. Let her think of walking out of their brand-
new marriage. Let her think of anything she liked—if she
could.

But all she would be capable of thinking about, he knew,
with every fibre of his being, would be him and him alone.

He let his hands fall to his sides. She was resisting him—
she would do so no longer. Swiftly he crossed to the banks of
wardrobes lining the side of the room, throwing open one door
after another until he found what he was looking for. Then,
grasping delicate folds, he tossed it at her.

'Go and change!'

He nodded towards the *en suite* bathroom. Andrea looked at
the garment he had thrown her. She knew what it was—the
negligee he had bought her in the shop that had treated her like
a rich man's floozy.

She turned and walked into the bathroom. Well, in a few minutes now she would be a rich man's unwanted wife.

The knowledge stabbed at her. It hurt—it hurt more than she had ever dreamt it could. Knowing what was coming. Knowing that she was to be Nikos Vassilis's oh-so-unwanted wife.

But it was inevitable. Had been from the moment he had looked across her grandfather's terrace at her and she had seen the flare of sexual interest in his eyes—felt it set light in her an answering flame.

Time to douse the fires.

Permanently.

She hugged the carapace to her more tightly than ever.

As the bathroom door clicked behind her Nikos got busy. Ringing for a steward, he had the scarcely touched bottle of champagne brought to him, and let the man turn down the bed. Then, retiring to the matching *en suite* bathroom he prepared himself. He had already shaved before dinner, and now it was a matter of moments to strip off and don a bathrobe.

He was already aroused. His celibacy of the last few weeks was obviously being felt—protestingly—by his body. He found himself thinking back to when he'd first thought through the implications of marrying Yiorgos Coustakis's unknown grand-daughter. He had worried about her lack of looks, her virginity, the fact that he would have to steel himself to get through his wedding night while making it as physically painless as possible for his dutiful bride.

His mouth twisted. Well, that was one word he didn't have to apply to Andrea! Dutiful she was not!

Would you want her to be? came the immediate ironic question, and the answer was immediate. No way! What he wanted her to be was…passionate, ardent, melting, molten, sensual, arousing, scorching, purring…

The litany went on inside his head, each word an image that burned with increasing fire in his guts. *Theos*, he wanted her! Wanted her as he wanted no other woman!

As an academic exercise he tried to make himself remember

what Xanthe looked like, Esme—but he could not do it. There was only one face, one body that he could see.

Andrea's.

My wife.

Possession surged through him. He was about to make her his in very truth, physically merging their bodies into one.

Desire kicked at him again, more urgent than ever.

With a tug he opened a shallow drawer in the vanity unit and drew out a handful of the small silvery packets that nestled within. He gave a wolfish grin. Oh, he'd get through the lot of them tonight, he thought.

He felt his body tighten. Sexual anticipation flooded him.

He strode out of the bathroom.

She was there, waiting for him. His breath caught.

Beautiful! His body jerked in salute of the image she made.

She stood in the centre of the room like a flame-haired queen. Her glorious locks were loose, tumbling down over her shoulders. The white, almost transparent silk of her negligee outlined her body, her full breasts thrust forward, straining against the taut material.

Desire kicked in him, hard and insistent.

'You're so beautiful—'

His voice was husky.

Andrea heard it, heard the note of raw desire in it. Her breath caught, and a shot of pure adrenaline surged through her. Then the words he had uttered penetrated, and the rush died, draining away like dirty oil from the sump of a wrecked car.

You're so beautiful...

Her mouth made a tight twist, and her eyes took on a strange brightness.

'Am I? Am I beautiful?'

Her voice was as strange as the twist to her mouth, the brightness of her eyes. She spoke to him, spoke to the man who stood waiting for her, stripped and ready for action.

A man who made her feel weak all over, inside and out, who made her heart clench and her breath catch just with looking at him.

But now it was him looking at her. She let him look. Wanted him to look.

That was the only way she could play this now—nothing else had worked. This must. It could not fail.

She went on speaking in that low, strange voice.

'This is what you want, isn't it, Nikos? A beautiful woman in your bed. Am I beautiful enough, Nikos? Am I?'

Her hands slid around the nape of her neck, lifting up her hair. She moved her head so that the glorious tumble flamed like fire. Then her hands slid down to the bodice of her negligee, fingers sliding beneath the delicate expensive material. She slipped it back, baring her shoulders, her hands grazing her breasts.

And all the time her eyes held his, never letting them go for a second.

'Am I beautiful, Nikos? Your beautiful bride?'

He couldn't answer her. His breath was frozen in his throat, though in his veins the blood roared.

She smiled. A fey, taunting smile.

Inside her head, behind the mask of her face, she was filled with flat, cold desolation. She was being cruel, she knew, but it was the only way. The only way.

She moved towards the bed, gliding softly, and lay down upon it, one hand loosely gathering the half-discarded material of her negligee to her breasts, the other smoothing the silk along the line of her legs.

'Am I your beautiful bride, Nikos? Beautiful enough for your bed?'

He came towards her. Purpose, desire, arousal—all in his eyes, his face—his ready, hungry body.

He could not resist her! Not for a second longer! Tumult consumed him. Who was this woman? One moment a cold, sulking ice-maiden, denouncing him for his sexual appetites, icily demanding a divorce before the ink was dry on the marriage certificate, sneering at him for his lowly origins. And now—now she was lying here, eternal Eve, displaying her body for him, lush and beautiful, oh, so beautiful, tempting him, arousing him—inviting him.

He looked down at her, caught in a pool of light, her body on show for him, veiled only by the sheerest of fabrics.

'Show me your body, Andrea—'

It was a rasp, a husk—a command, a plea.

There was a brightness in her eyes, a strangeness to her lips. He did not see it, saw only the soft outline of her limbs, her breasts, her belly...

'Show me...'

Her hand moved on her thigh, sliding the silk away, letting it slither from her thighs to the bedclothes on either side.

She looked at him. There was no expression in her eyes. None at all.

There was silence. A silence so profound Nikos knew he could hear his own heart beating.

Oh, dear God, dear God...

He stared down, the twisted, pitted surface of her legs scarring into his retinas as deeply as the scars that gouged and knotted her limbs from hip to ankle, runnelling through her wasted muscles, winding around her legs like some hideous net.

Horror drowned through him. She saw it in his face, his eyes. The brightness in her own eyes burned like acid. The tightness in her throat was like a drawn wire. Then deliberately, jerkily, she covered her legs again and stood up.

He stood aside to let her get to her feet. She yanked the negligee back into place over her shoulders, tugging at the belt to make it tighter—hugging her carapace into place. She must not lose it now. She must not.

'The comedy is ended,' she announced. Her voice was flat. 'I'll sleep in another room tonight. If you could be so good as to ensure we dock back at Piraeus tomorrow, I'll make my own way to the airport.'

She turned to go.

He caught her arm.

She looked down to where his fingers closed around her flesh.

'Let me go, Nikos. There's no need to say anything. Not a thing. I'm—sorry—it came to this. I thought it wouldn't be necessary. That you would accept the dissolution of our ridiculous marriage without any need to get this far. But in the end—' her voice tightened yet another unbearable notch '—it seemed the quickest way to convince you. Now, please let me go. I'll get my things and find another room…cabin…whatever they're called on a boat like this.'

He let her go, but only to slide his hand past her wrist and take her hand.

It was strange, thought Andrea, with the part of her mind where her act did not seem to work. The feel of his fingers wrapping hers was making her feel very strange. Very strange indeed.

He sat down on the edge of the bed, drawing her down beside him. His hand did not let go of hers.

'What happened, Andrea?' he asked.

There was something in his voice that made her eyes blink. The acid was burning them and she couldn't see properly. Something was misting her vision.

'What happened?' he asked again. His voice was very quiet.

She stared down at the carpet. There was a gold swirling in the pattern. It shifted in and out of focus. It seemed very important that it stay in focus. She stared at it again.

After a while, she spoke.

'It was a car crash, when I was fifteen. The older brother of one of my classmates was driving. He was driving us home— we'd been to the movies. I—I don't remember much. We swerved suddenly—a tyre burst, apparently—glass on the road, a broken bottle or something—and hit a wall. I was in the passenger seat. I was knocked out. I got trapped. The firemen had to cut me out. My legs were all smashed up. In hospital…in hospital…the doctors wanted…wanted…' Her voice was dry. 'They wanted to amputate—they said they were so smashed up they couldn't save them.'

She didn't hear the indrawn breath from the man sitting beside her. Nor did she feel the sudden tightening of his grip on her hand.

She went on staring at the carpet.

'My mother wouldn't let them. She said they had to save them. Had to. So—so they did. It…it took a long time. I was in hospital for months. Everything got pinned together somehow, and then, eventually, I was allowed into a wheelchair. They said I'd never walk. So much had gone. But Mum said I was going to walk. She said I had to. Had to. So…so I learned to walk again. I got sent to a special place where they help you learn to use your body again. It took a long time. Then they sent me for more operations, and that set me back, but Mum said it didn't matter, because I was going to walk again. I had to. And I did.'

The pattern in the carpet was going out of focus again. She swallowed.

'The only thing is, I can't do things like…like dance, and so on. It…it hurts. And I get frightened I'll damage them somehow. And though I can swim—it was part of my physio and still is, because the water helps to take the weight off my legs as I exercise them—I do it very early in the morning, when no one can…no one can see me.'

She blinked. 'I'm very lucky. Incredibly lucky. I learnt that in hospital, and in the physio place. There were others much worse off than me. Now the only thing wrong with me is that I have to be careful and not overdo things. And never marrying—' Her voice shook, but she steeled it to be still, and carried on. 'Never marrying won't be so bad. I've accepted that. I know no man can want me, not when they know, not when they've seen—'

Her voice broke.

Quietly, Nikos slid his hand out of hers. Then, just as quietly, he slipped to his knees on the floor at her feet. The dark of his head gleamed like black satin. He put his hands on her thighs. Beneath the flawless silk of the negligee he could feel the surface of her legs, uneven and knotted. Slowly he pushed the material aside.

She tried to stop him, tried to jerk her legs away from him, but his hands pressed on the sides of her thighs. His head bowed.

Slowly, infinitely slowly, Nikos let his hands move with absolute gentleness over the scarred, runnelled tissue of her legs, across the twisted muscles of her thighs, down over the knife-cut knees, along the warped, lumpen line of her calves, to circle her ankles. Then slowly, infinitely slowly, with the same absolute gentleness, he moved his hands back up, to rest once more on the sides of her thighs.

Then he lowered his mouth to her legs and kissed them—each thigh, each knee.

She sat still, so utterly still. All that moved within her body was her heart. She could not breathe; she could not think. Could not understand.

How can he touch them? How can he not be revolted? Disgusted?

A cruel memory surfaced in her thoughts. His name had been Dave, and he'd had a reputation with the girls. He'd made a play for her the moment he'd set eyes on her, and her refusal to go out with him had only made him more determined. She'd been twenty-two, and by then she had known just how ugly her legs were going to be all her life. She'd been chary of men. But Dave had gone on at her and on at her, and he was good-looking, with winning ways, and she couldn't help but fancy him, and in the end she'd given in to temptation and gone out with him. She'd wanted so much to be normal again—have boyfriends, discover sex. Fall in love. They'd dated quite a while, and he hadn't seemed to mind that she couldn't go clubbing, and she'd even, after a few weeks, told him about her accident. He hadn't seemed to mind.

Until the night she'd finally decided that twenty-two was no age to be a virgin still, and Dave had wanted her, so very, very much...

She could remember the look on his face as if it was yesterday. The strangled noise in his throat as she took her jeans off in his flat, the undisguised expletive that exploded from him. The word he'd called her.

Freak.

Crippled freak.

It's what I am. What every man will think me...

'Nikos—'

She caught his head with her hands. His hair was like black silk to her touch.

'Nikos—don't, please—'

He raised his mouth, lifting his face to her.

'Hush, *agape mou*, hush.' His voice was low.

He slipped his forearms underneath her thighs, and with the lightest exertion swung her legs round and on to the bed, following them himself to lie beside her. He leaned over her as she lay there, eyes wide and confused.

'Nikos—' Her voice was faint

He laid a finger over her mouth.

'This is not a time for talking,' he told her.

Then slowly, sensually, he began to make love to her.

It was like walking along the blade of a knife. Every move, every gesture, every touch was crucial. Control beaded in every nerve.

This is for her, not for you—

Carefully, incredibly carefully, Nikos kissed her. His mouth was light, as light as swansdown, his lips feathering hers, his tongue flickering at the corners of her mouth until it opened to him, and then slowly, delicately, he explored within.

Her eyes had shut. He hadn't noticed when, but it didn't matter. He knew she could not help it. Knew that the only way she could accept what was happening to her was by closing herself to everything but sensation—pure, blissful sensation.

And it was the same for him. He too knew that he must focus only and absolutely on what was happening now. Not just because of the utter physical control he had to impose on himself, but because somewhere, deep down inside, emotions were running so deep he could not name them. All but one.

Anger. Anger at a universe where such things happened. Anger at himself for being such a boor, a fool. Anger, most of all, at the men who had looked at her and let her feel that she was repulsive to them...

His mouth glided down the smooth, flawless column of her throat, seeking the hollow at its base where her pulse throbbed. With the skill of all his years he parted her robe, shaping delicately, sensuously, the sweet richness of her breasts. His mouth moved to their reddened tips and his tongue flickered over the hardening peaks.

Her heard her gasp, low in her throat, felt her head roll back as she savoured the sensations he aroused in her.

His body surged, and he quelled it urgently. He wanted— *Theos* how he wanted—to take her swollen nipple into his mouth, to suck and take his fill, move his body over hers at once, fill her with his, and feed and sate his appetite on her.

This is for her, not you—

With extreme control he held back, focussing only on her response, compressing her ripe breasts together so that his tongue could move from one peak to the other, endlessly keeping both in straining engorgement while little moans pulsed in her throat.

He felt her fingers come around his shoulders, beneath the towelling of his robe, pushing it back, sliding it from him, seeking the broad swathe of his shoulderblade to press into the smooth, flawless flesh of his back. He eased the robe from him to let her access him, never for a moment lifting his mouth away from her, only letting it drift down, over the swell of her breast, to lave the suddenly tautened plane of her belly.

And soon beyond.

As his fingers began to thread, tantalisingly, oh, so tantalisingly, in the tight curls that nested above the vee of her legs, Andrea thought she could stand no more. The sensation overload of her whole body was so intense, so exquisite she could not bear it.

But she could not escape it. It was like being sucked into a dark, breathless whirlpool, circling with infinite slowness, infinite power. She knew she ought to open her eyes, but she could not. Knew she ought to stop this, now, right now, push away those hands, that mouth…

But she could not. She was drowning in sensation, lost to all reason. There was nothing, nothing in the universe except what she was feeling now—as if her whole body were one whole, sweet mesh of soft, liquid pleasure that suffused every cell, every fibre of her being.

A pleasure that was growing with a mute, remorseless crescendo, spreading out in one sweet wave after another, quivering down all her nerves, washing through and through her as the slow, dark whirlpool took her with it.

His mouth was where his fingertips had been, and now his fingertips had moved on, brushing down the tender flesh on either side of the tightly curling nest of hair, seeking the parting of her legs.

Almost she tensed. Almost she thrust him back—away. Almost the knowledge of her disfigurement triumphed. But then, with a breathless sigh of pleasure, she felt her thighs loosen, fall open.

The whorls of pleasure intensified. She was weightless, floating in some sea of bliss that took everything away but the flickering of his tongue, the soft easing of his fingertip through folds made satin with a dew that his touch drew out of her.

The sensation was all there was.

Nothing had felt like this. Nothing in all her life. She had not known such sensation could exist.

A long, sweet moan escaped her. Her head rolled back, shoulders almost lifting from the bedclothes. The flickering intensified, the stroking fingertip easing her lips apart, exposing new, sweet feminine flesh to his skilled, exquisite touch.

Her hands clenched in the bedcover and she moaned again. Sensation broke over her again, wave after wave. And yet, with an instinct she did not know existed, she knew she was not yet sated. These were just the shallows of sensation.

She felt her hips lift and strain towards him, seeking more—more.

He answered her supplication. His fingertip drew back, gliding delicately in the flooding dew, circling slowly, rhythmically, like the vortex of a whirlpool, at the entrance to her body. Her fingers clenched again into the heavy folds of the bedspread, and her hips called to him again.

His tongue hovered minutely, and then, as the most drowning sensation yet broke through her, its very tip touched at the part that had swollen, all unbeknownst to her, past the protective furrow which had sheltered it.

Her breath caught, lips parting. What she had felt till now had been an echo, a shadow. Now, *now* was the true flame to her body lit. It burned beneath his touch, like a sweet, intense fire, making her whole body molten, focussing her entire being, as through a burning lens, on that single point of heat. It grew, and grew. She did not know how, or why—could feel nothing now, not the closeness of his body, nor the ministrations of his fingertip circling steadily, steadily, as her body opened to him, nor even the controlled, oh, so controlled accuracy of the flickering of his tongue, just there, just *there*, until the heat there, just *there*, was all there was, all there could ever be.

She was molten, molten, the warmth welling from the only centre of her body that could exist now, until it ascended through every vein, higher, ever higher, as the whirlpool sucked at her and sucked, and she could hear, from far, far way, a long, slow, rising cry that came from somewhere so deep inside she had never known its existence, reaching out, reaching out to exhale through her lifted, opening mouth...

Heat flooded through her, a huge, overwhelming sheet of flame that simply raced to encompass her whole body. It flooded again and again—a surge of flame, lifting her body, arching her spine, her neck, a surge of pleasure so intense, so absolute, it filled her with incredulity and awe that her body could feel so much...so much.

And go on feeling. It came, wave after wave, one more bliss-

ful than the next, and the cry from the heart of her being went
on, and on, and on...

She could feel the internal muscles of her body rippling inside her, feel the blood surging, feel the pulsing of every fold,
the rush of moisture releasing.

Time lost all meaning as she gave herself, consumed, to the
molten overflow flooding and flooding again through her. And
still it came. Until, singing its ecstasy, her ecstasy, her body
began, finally to ebb, exhausted, sated, the vast, encompassing
whirlpool slowly, slowly stilling...

Arms were holding her. There was the alien scent of male-
ness, the strong hardness of masculine muscles, the brush of
body hair against the new softness of her breasts. She was
folded into it. Folded against him.

Slowly reality came back to her, and she realised what had
happened.

Andrea lay in his arms as motionless as a rag doll. Her entire
body was limp. He was not surprised. When she had peaked it
had been like an endless outpouring of her whole body, the
flush of ecstasy suffusing the paleness of her skin, her eyes
fluttering beneath her long, long lashes, her breath exhaling in
a long, slow susurration of bliss.

And now she lay in the sheltering circle of his arms.

Nikos held her quietly, not moving, not stirring, knowing his
own body was at peace as well.

And more than his body.

He had done the right thing, he knew. Followed his uncon-
scious instinct—knowing, somehow, that he must take her on
a journey she needed to make. A journey that must be an ex-
orcism of all her fears, a healing of the wounds that had been
laid upon her.

He felt the inert length of her legs beside him and coldness
iced through him. He heard her words again—*The doctors
wanted to amputate...*

Inside his head he heard his answering cry of negation of
such a fate.

'Andrea mou…' He did not know if he said the words aloud or not. But they echoed in him all the same.

His eyes were heavy. At his side, in the cradle of his arms, he felt her body slacken imperceptibly, saw her face slide into repose, her breath shallowing into sleep. He felt its call, his eyelids too heavy to hold apart, and as his own breathing slowed his muscles relaxed, like hers, into the sweet embrace of sleep as well.

CHAPTER NINE

THERE was sunlight in the room, bright and pouring, flooding in from the wide-set windows. Andrea stirred, surfacing unwillingly from sleep. There was some reason she didn't want to wake up, but she didn't want to think about what that might be.

But wake she must. Someone was shaking her shoulder. Not roughly, but insistently.

'Andrea, *mou*, we are wasting a glorious day! Come, breakfast awaits.'

Nikos's voice was a mix of chiding and encouraging, his tone deliberately light. It would be the best way to play it, he knew. For the moment at least. She didn't want to move, didn't want to acknowledge his existence, but she must—this was not something she could run away from or deny any longer. He would not hurry her, he would be as gentle as she needed, but her denial must end. He desired her and she desired him—and the trifle of her scarred legs must not get in the way of her acceptance of that inalienable truth.

He dropped a kiss on her exposed cheek.

'What do you say in English? Lazybones?' He stood up. 'There is a pot of tea for you here to wake you up—the chef poured all his genius into making you the perfect English "cuppa"—you must not offend him by rejecting it! He will sulk for days and we shall starve! So, drink your tea like a good girl, and come and join me on deck in fifteen minutes.' He stooped briefly, to brush her cheek very softly with his fingers. 'It will be all right, Andrea—trust me.'

Then he was gone.

She needed every one of those fifteen minutes he had allowed her. As she showered and dressed a single thought drummed through her brain—*Don't think about it! Just don't think about it!*

But the moment she emerged onto the sunlit deck, where a breakfast table was set up, and laid eyes on Nikos sitting there it was all for nothing. Memory, in total, absolute detail, came flooding back to her.

He could see it in her face, her eyes, and acted immediately. He got up and came across to her swiftly, taking her hands.

'Come—breakfast,' he said. 'What would you like to have?' He swept an arm to indicate a sideboard groaning with enough food to feed an army, with everything on it from fresh fruit to devilled kidneys.

Grateful, as he had intended, for the banality of choosing something to eat, she let him help her to lightly scrambled eggs, toast, and a plate of highly scented freshly cut pineapple. She felt surprisingly hungry.

If I don't think about it, it never happened... she told herself, sitting herself down at the table.

There were no crew in sight, and she was grateful for that too. Whether it was Nikos being tactful she didn't know, but she simply couldn't have borne to have that mute chorus in attendance.

Instead, she looked about her. The deck they were seated on faced the stern, and all Andrea could see all around was a glorious expanse of sparkling blue water. The sight lifted her spirits of its own accord. A tiny breeze whisked around her cheeks, fanning the tendrils of her hair. It was a bright, fresh, brand-new day.

From nowhere, absolutely nowhere, a sense of wellbeing filled her. It was illogical, impossible, but it was there. She felt her spirits lighten. Who could be otherwise on a morning like this?

She set to, demolishing her breakfast swiftly. She'd only picked at her food over that excruciating dinner last night, and now she was making up for it. There was something so incredibly comforting about scrambled eggs on toast...

Nikos said nothing, just busied himself leafing through a

newspaper as he worked steadily through a surprisingly hearty breakfast. As they ate, with him paying her no more attention than from time to time checking if she would like more tea, more toast, more butter, little by little she found herself capable of lifting her eyes from her food, and instead of sliding them immediately to the sparkling horizon let them pass, in focus, over the man sitting opposite her.

Don't think about it! she reminded herself, and to her surprise the technique seemed to work.

Maybe it was because Nikos seemed so totally relaxed. He sat there, a man at peace with the world, eating his breakfast beneath an Aegean sky. Maybe too, Andrea realised, it was because for the first time she was seeing him in informal clothes. Instead of the habitual business suit or evening dress this morning he was wearing a beautifully cut but informally tailored short-sleeved, open-necked fawn-coloured shirt and tan-coloured chinos.

He still looked devastating, of course, but the air of command was absent—or, if not absent, definitely off-duty.

As he swallowed the last of his coffee, folded up his newspaper and glanced towards her some twenty minutes later she realised she was just sitting there, her own breakfast finished, content to feel the warm sun on her face, the air ruffling her hair occasionally, and watch the stern flag flap in the breeze.

It dawned on her that they were not moving.

'Where are we?' she asked, puzzled. 'Why have we stopped?'

'We are on the approach to Heraklion. If you wish, we can make landfall.'

'Heraklion?' queried Andrea. 'Isn't that on Crete?'

'Yes. The island is visible from the aft. Shall we go and look?'

There didn't seem to be a particularly good reason not to, and Andrea found herself standing up as Nikos moved to draw back her chair. She walked beside him along the side of the vessel, and as they drew clear onto the foredeck she could see the long east-west land mass of Greece's largest island lying to the south of them. Mountains rose in the interior, almost all along the spine of the island, and Nikos pointed to the town of Heraklion on the coast in front of them.

'Knossos is only a few kilometres inland. Would you like to go and visit the Minotaur?' he asked genially.

The prospect tugged at her. Then, sinkingly, she realised she must ask for the yacht to put about and return to Piraeus. She had a plane to catch.

As if reading her thoughts, Nikos touched her arm lightly. Though it was only the briefest gesture, she felt her skin tingle.

'Stay a little, Andrea *mou*. What harm will it do, after all?'

His voice was light, but there was a cajoling beneath the lightness. 'Today we could just play tourists. It's been a strain, these last weeks—let us relax a little, *ne*?'

She tried to answer, but couldn't. If she answered him she would have to open that door that she had banged tightly shut this morning as she got out of bed. And she couldn't face that.

The alternative was to go on along this path she was on now. It would be temptingly easy to do so.

She had never seen Knossos, and was unlikely ever to get the opportunity to do so again. Just as she had wanted to see Athens while she was there, now she wanted to see the famous site of the very first civilisation Europe could boast, the Minoans, whose vast, labyrinthine Bronze Age palace at Knossos made the Parthenon look modern.

And see it she did, joining the throng of tourists who poured over the massive remains of the excavated and partially restored site, amazed at the sheer size of a palace first built over four thousand years ago and destroyed so cataclysmically. She was both fascinated and awestruck—and saddened. The exquisite murals, even if restored, caught at a world where militarism and armaments seemed quite absent—a world where nature and fertility were more valued than war and conquest.

'They did not need military might—all the Minoan palace sites lack ramparts,' Nikos reminded her when she found herself remarking on it. 'Theirs was a maritime trading empire, a thalassocracy, linking Egypt, the Levant, Asia Minor and Greece. And, of course, the legend of the annual tribute of seven youths and seven maidens to feed to the Minotaur, so central to the story of the gallant Theseus, more likely represents the tribute the ancient mainland Greeks, the Myceneans, were required to pay the Minoans. It was more likely commercial rivalry that brought down the Minoan empire, not the death of a monster!'

'And the earthquakes and tidal waves,' added Andrea. 'How terrible it must have been!' She shuddered, remembering a television programme she had once watched which had recreated, with computer simulation, the terrifying volcanic explosion of the island of Thera, modern Santorini, which had blasted the atmosphere with dark, choking, poisonous dust and sent a wall of water hurtling south to crash devastatingly upon the low, defenceless Cretan shore.

She looked around her. All about had once been walls and rooms, stairs and chambers, courtyards and gardens, storerooms and towers, bustling with people carrying on their ordinary, everyday lives. All gone now. All silenced.

They were once as alive as you are now. Felt the warmth of the same sun upon their faces, felt the same earth beneath their feet as you do now.

As if he could read her thoughts on her face, she heard Nikos say quietly at her side, 'We must live while we can, Andrea. We have no other choice except to make the most of what is given to us. Our minds, our hearts—our bodies and our passions.'

For a moment, the briefest moment, she met his eyes and read what was in them. Then, his message sent, he lightened his expression.

'Are you hungry? Let us eat.'

They lunched, at Andrea's instigation, at a small tourist restaurant close to the palace of Knossos, which, though clearly catering for the masses, appealed to her with its vine-dappled terrace set back, overlooking the road. It was pretty, and quite unpretentious, and they both ate a typical tourist salad of feta cheese and tomatoes drizzled in olive oil, followed by the ultimate Greek tourist dish of lamb kebabs.

If Nikos was taken aback by her choice, he hid it. Maybe after a lifetime of eating only in the most expensive restaurants it was amusing for her to eat such humble fare and mingle with ordinary folk whose grandfathers were not multimillionaires.

She looked quite natural in such a place, he suddenly realised. Her hair was drawn back into a simple plait, and if he did not know better he'd have said that her clothes—jeans and a simple white T-shirt—could easily have come out of a chainstore. She must be favouring a designer who charged a fortune to achieve that very effect.

Nor did she balk in the slightest at the taste of the robust but rough Domestica wine she drank. To Nikos it brought back memories from his early years, before his palate had become exposed only to the finest vintages. He wondered when it was that he had last drunk such table wine as now filled his glass.

Too long. The words echoed inside his head, and he put them aside with a frown.

'Where would you like to go this afternoon?' he asked, to change his thoughts. 'Shall we drive to a beach and sun ourselves?'

Immediately he cursed himself. In his head he heard her low words, filled with quiet, unemotional anguish, saying how she only swam very early in the morning, when no one could see her legs...

'Or perhaps you would like to see Heraklion?' he hurried on. 'Or we could drive further into the interior, perhaps? There is Mount Ida to see, where the god Zeus is said to have been born, in a cavern there.'

'I'd like that,' Andrea replied. 'I...I'm not sure I'm up to much more walking, I'm afraid. I'm rather feeling it in my legs after tramping around Knossos. Not that I'd have missed it for the world!' she added, lest she sound whining.

'I'll phone for the car,' said Nikos, and got out his mobile phone to summon the large, chauffeur-driven hire car that had brought them here from the yacht and which was now parked in the palace car park.

'Nikos—' She stayed his hand and he stopped, surprised. 'I—I don't suppose,' she found herself saying wistfully, 'it would be possible—if not today, then perhaps tomorrow—if we are still here, of course,' she burbled, feeling awkward suddenly, 'to have a car like that one there to drive around in, would it?'

She pointed down to where one of the legion of open-sided four-by-fours, favoured by tourists as hire cars, was making its way along the road.

'They look such fun,' she said.

They *were* fun, she discovered shortly. For the first time it dawned on her that being the wife of a rich man—however fraudulently, to her mind, and certainly however temporarily—had its compensations. A swift phone conversation with the chauffeur and the luxury limo had been traded for a self-drive bouncing Jeep.

She had to hang on tight, especially as they started to climb into the central Cretan mountains. The hairpin bends were tight, and got tighter, but as they did the views got more and more stupendous. The mildness of the lowland air crispened into a clarity that cleansed the lungs.

'This is wonderful! Thank you!'

They had stopped at a viewpoint and were looking down over the island, towards the sea beyond. Forested slopes spread out like skirts around them.

'I am glad you are enjoying yourself, *agape mou*.'

He smiled down at her. Again, as in the aftermath of the concert, there was nothing in Nikos's reply except open appreciation of her gratitude for showing her Crete.

She smiled back up at him, her eyes warm, and in that moment she saw his expression change, as if her smile had done something to him.

Hurriedly she looked away, saying the first thing that came into her head.

'For a Greek island, Crete is very forested,' she observed.

'It was not always so,' he answered, accepting her gambit.
He must go slowly—oh, so slowly—with this wounded deer,
lest she flee him and wound herself even more in the process.
'When the Venetians ruled Crete, and then the Turks, much of
the forest was cut down for timber for ships. In those days
public enemy number one for trees were mountain goats, who
ate the saplings before they could mature. So a decree went
out offering a bounty for every dead goat brought down from
the mountains.' His voice became very dry. 'It is perhaps pre-
dictable to relate that an active goat-breeding programme was
soon well underway amongst the impoverished but financially
astute mountain-dwelling peasants...'

She laughed, as he had intended.

'The best-laid plans of bureaucrats,' she commented, equally
dryly.

He slipped his hand into hers, making the movement very
casual. 'Indeed. Come—back on the road again. Finding a café
would be very welcome, ne?'

They stopped for coffee at a little *cafeneion* perched precari-
ously, so it seemed to Andrea, over the side of a precipitous
slope. The view, however, more than made up for it. They sat
in silence, absorbing the peace and serenity around them, but
it was a silence a world away from the silence at dinner the
night before, Andrea found herself thinking. Then it had all
been strain and horribleness. Now—now it was...com-
panionable.

The thought was odd. Almost unbelievable.

As she sat there, sipping her western filter coffee while
Nikos drank the undrinkable treacly brew of the native, she
decided she did not want to think about it.

She just wanted to enjoy the moment. For now, it was
enough.

It was early evening by the time they got back to the coast.
They did not arrive back at Heraklion, but further west, at
Rethimnon.

'Just in time for us to make our *volta*,' said Nikos.

'*Volta?*'

'In the early evening, after work and before dinner, we take our stroll around the town—to see and be seen,' explained Nikos.

With the westering sun turning the azure sea to turquoise, and yellowing the limestone buildings around the pretty Venetian harbour of the town, it was a pleasant thing to do, discovered Andrea. They strolled around the quayside. And if at some point Nikos slipped his arm around Andrea's shoulders, to shield her from a group of lively tourists heading in the opposite direction, she found, when he did not remove it, that she did not mind. Indeed, the opposite was true. The warmth of his casual embrace was comforting. And when, as they took their places at a table set out on the quayside to have a drink, he let go of her, she felt, she realised, strangely bereft.

Nikos took a beer, Andrea a tall glass of fruit juice, and they watched the world go by. It was very easy, very relaxed. They talked about Crete—its long struggle for independence, its ordeals under Nazi occupation, and its modern Renaissance as a tourist destination. Neutral subjects. Safe subjects.

'Do you know the island well?' she asked.

He shook his head. 'I'm afraid my visits have mostly been brief, and in respect of business. I've seen more of Crete today than ever before.' He paused, then said with deliberate casualness, 'Shall we stay a few days longer?'

She stilled. 'I—I...'

He covered her hand with his. 'You do not need to decide now, Andrea *mou*. Let us take things as they come, *ne*?'

There was meaning in his words, but she could not challenge him. Instead she looked out over the gilded water, streaming with the setting sun.

'Shouldn't we start heading back to Heraklion? Won't they be wondering where we are?'

He gave a laugh. 'Captain Petrachos sailed the yacht along the coast—he's anchored off the shore now. We'll take a launch back to it whenever we want. There's no hurry.'

'Oh,' said Andrea. Once again she realised how very, very

easy being a holidaymaker was if you had a luxury yacht trailing around after you.

'Shall we dine ashore?' enquired Nikos, calling for another beer.

'Can we?'

He laughed again. 'Andrea, this is our hon—' He caught himself, and amended his words. 'Our holiday—we can do anything we like!'

Andrea looked around. Everywhere were open-fronted restaurants, tables spilling out onto the quayside and the pavements, happy holidaymakers enjoying their escape from humdrum lives. It was livening up now, and she could hear the throb of bazouki music emanating from the bars.

'Let's eat here!' she enthused. She could not face returning to that opulent monstrosity of a yacht, whose garish luxury appalled her so. Besides, she felt safe here, amongst so many people....

And Nikos was being so *nice*...

She sipped her orange juice, nibbling moist, succulent olives out of the dish placed in front of them, staring out over the harbour. Carefully, tremulously, she opened her mind and let herself face up to what had happened.

Nikos had made love to her. He had taken her naked body and brought it to ecstasy. Initiated her into the realm of sensual experience. Changed her from an unknowing, virginal maiden into a woman who knew the power of the senses. The overwhelming, irresistible power that took away all reason, all logic, and swept her away, to let her do things, experience things that she had never, ever thought to experience.

It happened. It was real. I let it happen.

She could have stopped him—*should* have stopped him— but she hadn't. She hadn't found the strength to stop him.

Even though she knew exactly why he had done what he had.

She said the words to herself, spelling them out. Letting there be no mistake about it. Refusing to deceive herself.

He made love to me. Last night Nikos made love to me be-cause he felt sorry for me.

That was the truth of it.

It tore at her, pulling her in two. Part of her was filled with mortification that this most perfect paean to masculine perfection should have had to force himself to make love to her scarred, disfigured body. But part of her was filled with wonder—wonder that a man who had married her for no other reason than to get her grandfather's business empire should have had the compassion, the kindness, to feel sorry for her...

Emotions stirred in her heart, welling up, but she knew they were dangerous. Very dangerous.

Nikos Vassilis, who had married the splendid Coustakis heiress, not the humble, ordinary Andrea Fraser, would have no use for such emotions—and neither must she.

It was late before they returned to the yacht. They had eaten in one of the harbourside restaurants, filled with chattering, cheerful tourists. It had been fun, and had distracted Andrea from her deeper thoughts. But now, as the motor launch creamed its way across the dark sea towards the string of lights that edged the massive bulk of her grandfather's latest toy, those thoughts surfaced.

Nikos could tell. As he helped her up the lowered steps to gain the safety of the deck he knew, by the way she immediately pulled her hand free of his, that she was filled with nervous self-consciousness.

Keep playing it easy, he adjured himself.

Dismissing the crewman with a smile, he turned to Andrea. 'Come, let us watch the night.'

He led her up to the uppermost deck, towards the stern. They would not be overlooked there. The bridge crew were out of sight, and he had given orders that the rest of the staff could stand down.

Glad for a reprieve from having to go to bed, and not having the faintest idea what on earth Nikos was going to do about sleeping arrangements now, Andrea followed him. It was, she had to admit, a glorious sight. The twinkling line of lights along the Cretan coast echoed the blaze of stars in the celestial oceans above their heads.

They stood side by side, leaning on the railings, trying to identify constellations.

'I only know the Plough and Orion in winter,' admitted Andrea. 'London isn't very good for star-gazing.'

'We should sleep in a goat hut on the top of Mount Ida to have the clearest view on the island!' teased Nikos, and she smiled.

'Crete was wonderful,' she said wistfully. 'Thank you for taking me there today.'

Lightly, very lightly, he slipped his hand underneath the plait of her hair at the back of her neck.

'As I said, *pethi mou*, we can spend as long as we like here. Shall we do that?'

His fingers were brushing her nape. Very lightly.

It set every nerve in her body quivering.

Danger!

You've got to stop this—now!

'Nikos—'

'Hmm?' His fingertips were playing with loose strands of hair. She felt ripples of sensation down her spine.

'Nikos—'

She paused again, trying to concentrate, trying to focus on what she had to tell him. *Must* tell him. Right now.

'I—I have to talk to you!' The words came out in a rush.

It did not stop his fingers gentling at the tender skin beneath her ear, nor did it stop the shivers of pleasure vibrating in her.

'What about?' he asked idly. His other hand had come around her spine to rest on her hip. It felt large, and heavy, and warm. And dangerous.

Still he went on feathering the loosening tendrils of her hair, brushing the velvet of her skin.

She forced herself to concentrate.

'About…about…what happened.'

'When?' asked Nikos, in that same lazy tone, as his thumb moved to brush along the line of her jaw.

'Last…last night….'

'Ahh,' breathed Nikos. 'That.'

'Yes! That!' echoed Andrea. It was supposed to come out forcefully, but as his thumb grazed the cleft of her chin it only came out as a sigh.

'This?' queried Nikos. His fingertips still stroked her cheek lightly, oh, so lightly, but now his thumb pressed lightly, oh, so lightly, on her full lower lip.

'No!'

'Ahh. Then *this*, perhaps…'

His hand smoothed over her hip languorously, shaping its feminine contour with lazy ease.

She felt her muscles clench spasmodically, unable to control them. She could feel how close he was behind her now, his body almost encircling hers. How had he got so close suddenly?

She had no time to think of an answer.

'Oh,' he murmured, 'then it must be *this, ne*?'

His thumb pressed on her lower lip and slid into the moistness within, gliding along the tender inner surface.

Sensation shimmered at his velvet touch, vibrating through her like a siren call she could not resist—could not.

She moaned, and softly bit the fleshy pad, drawing it into her mouth to do so.

She could not help herself. She simply could not help herself.

She heard herself moan again, a little whimper in her throat, and now his hand was cupping her jaw, and his thumbpad was grazing the edge of her teeth.

She bit again, laving it with her tongue longingly, helplessly.

He turned her in his arms and kissed her properly.

She yielded without a word, her eyelids fluttering shut as she gave herself to the bliss of having Nikos kiss her.

It was a deep, sensual kiss. A kiss filled with all the hunger he had suppressed. A kiss for himself as well as her.

His arms slid around her, holding her tight against him, his hand spearing her hair, holding her head steady for him as he plundered the sweetness of her mouth, tongues mating and writhing.

Hunger flooded through her. Her body leapt in recognition of what was happening. This was no seduction. It was rediscovery. Glorious, potent rediscovery. Her hands wound around his neck, holding him to her, unable to let go—not while the hunger that suddenly seared within her was feeding on him, mouth to mouth, shaping and touching, wanting and needing...

Needing so much more... Wanting so much more...

Wanting everything. Wanting possession.

His possession. Nikos Vassilis. Only his.

Now—oh, right now...now...

Reality douched through her. She yanked away from him, breathless, horrified.

'Nikos! No!'

Her rejection was a gasp of disbelief that she had actually got to this point. She twisted free, backing away.

'No?' The tone was quizzically ironic. She did not see the control he had to use to maintain so light a voice.

'No,' she said again, more firmly now, swallowing, trying to still the frantic beating of her racing heart. Trying to find reason, logic, hard sense. 'You don't have to do this. I...I said we had to talk about...about last night, and we do—but it's just to say I understand. I know why you...why you did what you did. I accept that. You felt sorry for me. You felt sorry for me because you saw me as an object of pity. But it's OK—' she held her hand up '—it's OK. I understand.' She swallowed again. 'You don't have to feel you must give a repeat performance. I understand.'

As she spoke Nikos had leant back against the rails, resting his elbows on the guard rail.

'I'm glad you understand,' he said lightly. 'It was certainly the worst night of my life, I can tell you!'

He looked at her, watching her face change as she took in

what he had just said. There was a stricken look on it, but he ignored it.

'Yes,' he said again, 'certainly the worst night of my life.'

Andrea could feel her nails digging into her palms. Did he have to be so brutal about it? Did he have to ram home just how repugnant he had found the ordeal of making love to a freak? Her throat had tightened, wire pulling on it. Agonising. He was talking again. She could hardly bear to hear what he was saying. But the words penetrated all the same.

'I've never done what I had to do last night,' he told her. 'It was excruciating.'

The expression on her face was devastated, but he ploughed on. 'And I never, ever want to go through it again. I tell you—' he eyed her straight, and said what he had to say '—having to hold myself back like that was absolute agony. I was aching for you—totally bloody *aching* for you.' A long, shuddering sigh escaped him. '*Theos*, you've no idea what it was like, Andrea *mou*—having your fantastic, gorgeous body stripped naked and pulsing for me and not being able to possess you totally. God, it was hell—sheer hell!' He shook his head. 'Never again, I promise you—never again!'

He straightened suddenly, and rested his hand on either shoulder. 'But you needed your space, and I knew I owed you that. So...' He looked down at her, starlight in his eyes. 'Last night was your night, Andrea *mou*. But tonight—oh, tonight—' his voice had changed, husky suddenly '—tonight is *mine*...'

He pulled her into him, jerking her, and closed his mouth over hers. Then, with a rough, urgent motion, he swept her up into his arms and strode off with her, to make her his wife.

It was, she realised some eternity later, the rawness of his hunger, the voracity of his appetite that convinced her. As he tumbled her down upon their vast bed, coming down beside her and pinioning her hands either side of her head as he lowered his mouth to hers again to feed and feed upon her, she felt rush up from the depths of her being such a gladness, such a glory, she was breathless with it.

His mouth ravished hers, allowing her no quarter, no defence, and he overpowered her effortlessly, easily. She was a willing traitor, oh, so willing! His body arched over hers and her hands ran over the smoothness of his shirt, fumbling with buttons as, overcome with a desperate urge she had never felt before, never known existed, she longed frantically to feel his skin, his flesh, his muscle and sinew beneath her seeking hands.

He helped her—shucking off his shirt, peeling off her T-shirt while he did so, slipping the clasp on the back of her bra in one unseen skilful movement. Her breasts spilled free and she heard his throat rasp with pleasure at the sight before he buried his face in their ripeness, his questing mouth homing in on what he sought.

She gasped with pleasure as he suckled her, thrusting her breasts up, bearing down upon the bed with her hips, her shoulders. He fed voraciously, licking and sucking until her nipples were as solid as steel, radiating fiery points of pleasure fiercely through her body. Her hands roamed over the smooth steel of his back, glorying in the power of his perfect musculature, revelling in the feel of his body over hers.

He swept on, mouth racing down the flat, taut plane of her belly, tongue whirling within the secret of her navel even as he was urgently undoing the fastening of her jeans, sliding her zip open and then in the same movement sliding his hand inside. She gasped and roiled as a thousand fires lit where he touched.

Her heart was racing, thundering. There was no light in the room and she could not see its garish, tasteless opulence. She could feel only the satin of the bedclothes beneath her naked back, her naked bottom and thighs, for her jeans were gone and her panties too were tossed aside. Now Nikos was moving over her, and she realised that somehow, somehow, he was as naked as she.

She gloried in the feel of him, revelled in it, racing her hands all over his body. Flesh to flesh, skin to skin, mouth to mouth, hip to hip. She felt him straining at her, felt his engorged length against the softness of her belly, and the realisation, searing through her, sent a shockwave of exultation through her. He wanted her! Nikos wanted her! She knew it—knew it absolutely. Men could not fake it. Their desire, their lust, surged in their bodies, signalling the urgency of their passions.

Like an outgrown cloak her fears fell away from her, cast aside in the revelation, and in their place, released like a tiger from its cage, she was filled suddenly, desperately, with a longing so intense, a hunger so searing that her hand slid from gripping his shoulder as his mouth consumed hers down between their bodies to grasp him.

She wanted to feel him, strong and potent in her hand, his surging masculinity inflaming her with a hunger that only he could fulfil. She clasped him greedily, feeling the strength of him.

She heard him gasp with pleasure, sending a power-pulse of desire through her. She wanted to please him, wanted to give him pleasure now, right now, just as he was filling her with feelings, sensations that stormed within her, roiled and rocked her. She wanted him—wanted him to pierce and fill and stretch her, flood her with his seed, his very being.

'Nikos!' Her voice was a cry, a plea, an exultation.

He reared over her. '*Theos*, but I must have you!' His voice was a rasp of hunger, intensity. His hand caressed her belly, her thighs, then parted her legs for him. She guided him to her, heart pounding, blood surging in her veins, her body afire. She was flooding for him, her body straining to his, hips twisting and lifting to him, reaching for him, and then she felt, with a thrill that went through her whole body, that he was poised above her, ready to thrust and pierce her to the very core, her very heart.

'I must have you—'

The words grated from him and he took each of her hands, lifting and placing them each side of her head, pinioning them with his, holding her body still for him, spread for him, hips lifting to receive him.

She could feel the urgency of his need for her. Power surged through her. The power of her sex, flowering in a glorious, heady welling of sensation that fused her body to her mind, fused her aroused, throbbing flesh to the incandescence lighting her whole being.

She raised her mouth to his and bit softly, deliberately at his.

'Then take me,' she answered. 'Take me.'

He waited no longer. With slow descent he lowered his body into hers.

His control, his purpose was absolute. Her dew-drenched readied body parted for him, accepting him within her as a needed, hungered-for presence. She stretched around him, and as pain fluttered briefly, fleetingly, it was swept away by the drowning tide of exultation that consumed her as he made her his.

He filled her absolutely, and she gasped with the realisation that their bodies had fused, become one, pulsing, beating to the same single heartbeat that throbbed between them, sex to sex, thigh to thigh, palm to palm, pressing and joining.

Her mouth opened in a wondrous, wordless cry, neck arching back, hips lifting higher to meld their flesh together.

He was reared over her, fused within her, and she gloried in it. Around his manhood's strength her muscles clenched, holding him tightly, dearly, and the pressure of his body in hers thickened him in answer to her. It was all she needed. Like a long, slow wave her body detonated around his, sending a tidal pulse through all her flesh.

She buckled around him, every muscle straining, and the detonation came again, surging out like a shockwave.

She cried out, gasping, spine arching like a bow.

It was liquid pressure, liquid pleasure, so intense, so absolute that it shocked her even as it convulsed her. It flooded through her, reaching through every vein, every overloaded nerve-fibre, rushing out to fill her fingertips, her toes, flushing her body with its tide.

And behind it surged another tide, and yet another, and with one, wondering, stunned part of her mind she realised her body was resonating with another's. Nikos was gasping, surging, pulsing into her, and she was drawing him in, the tide convulsing her sucking him into her, possessing him utterly.

She heard him gasp, cry out in triumph, and the triumph was hers too, and his, and theirs, and still their bodies surged to the tidal wave carrying them on its endless bounty.

Her fingers clutched his, squeezing so tightly she could feel the slick between their joined palms seal them unbreakably, just as their bodies were joined—unbreakably.

Slowly, oh, so slowly, the tidal pulse began to ebb, draining deep away, back into the core, the heart of her body, where it had come from. Slowly, oh, so slowly, he lowered himself to her, to rest his exhausted, sated weight upon her, crush the slackening tissues of her breasts.

They were both panting, breathless with exertion, hearts thundering in their chests. His body covered hers, slick with sweat. Her hands slid free and came around his back, wrapping him to her. She could feel, against her own, his heartbeat slamming, then slowly, slowly, as the torpor of inertia took them over, it began to ease and lessen.

How long they lay like that, their bodies fast entwined, motionless with satiation and exhaustion, she did not know, could not tell. Time had no meaning any more. She had discovered eternity.

After a while, a long, endless while, he stirred. The sweat had dried on his back, and where her arms did not enfold him his skin was cold.

Heavily, he lifted his head from her shoulder.

She felt the movement of muscles in his back and instinctively tightened her grip around him.

He gave a laugh. A low, brief laugh.

'No, I, too, do not wish to move, Andrea *mou*, but yet we must.'

He managed to lever himself up to his elbows, making her slacken her grip on him so that only her hands could touch either side his spine.

'Come—I must tend to you.'

Carefully, he eased from her.

She felt bereft, empty, desolate. He slipped away from her in the dark and she heard him cross the carpeted floor. Then a door opened, and a light flooded briefly, before closing to dimness. She shut her eyes. Her heart was in tumult. But she could not think, could not reason. Could only lie and let the dimness close her round.

Exhaustion claimed her.

His footsteps crossing towards the bed roused her from the slumber she had sunk into. As she surfaced she could hear, she realised, the sound of water running. Before she realised what he was intending he scooped his hands underneath her and folded her up into his arms.

'I don't want you to feel sore, *pethi mou*,' he murmured, and took her through into the bathroom, lowering her gently into the swirling water in the huge, circular bath, foaming high with bubbles.

It was bliss of a different kind. She gave a sigh, and gave herself up to the warmth, pausing only to reach and twist her hair into a precarious self-fastened knot on top of her head. She closed her eyes and let the water swirl around her.

There seemed to be fine jets of water shushing out at her from all around, and she realised the huge bath must be some kind of Jacuzzi. As the tumult in her heart subsided, washed away by the warm, relaxing water, she felt for the first time the physical effects of what had happened to her. She eased her thighs, letting the water swirl gently, soothingly, around her ravished body.

'Are you in pain?'

Nikos's voice was concerned. She opened her eyes. He had not put on the central light in the bathroom, only the light above the mirror, so the brightness was mellow, not glaring. He had put on a bathrobe and was looking down at her, his hands plunged into its pockets.

She could not quite meet his eyes. Not yet.

'No, not pain, but...I feel...exercised.'

She caught his eye then, and suddenly there was an answering gleam in his.

'Oh, yes,' he answered softly. 'As do I, I assure you...'

He held her gaze, and the knowledge in his eyes flooded her. For a moment the mutual acknowledgement of what had happened flowed between them.

'Nikos, I—' she began—because she had to say *something*, she must.

He shook his head, silencing her. 'No. Say nothing. We will take this slowly, Andrea *mou*. As slowly as we need. Now—' he held up a hand '—I shall leave you in privacy a while. Relax and recover. Don't move until I come and get you.'

He left her in peace, the silence broken only by the occasional popping of a bubble. She felt—*fulfilled*, she realised, and a quiet wonder went through her to lie like a fine, rare sheen over her heart.

The warmth and the water, the silence and the solitude eased her, lapping her spent body. With a light tap to the door Nikos returned after a little while and helped her out of the bath, enveloping her in a huge fleecy bathtowel. She was almost asleep, and he could see that all she would do now was rest for the remainder of the night.

He gave a private rueful smile. He could have kept going all night, but for now he must let her set the pace. She had entered a new kingdom—he must give her time to take possession of it, to know its ways and passions.

So he simply lifted her off her feet, carrying her back to the bed like a swaddled baby, and set her down between smooth satin sheets, gently drawing the towel off her. The satin felt cold to her skin, and when he returned from the bathroom a moment later, and turned off the night, she welcomed the warmth of his encircling embrace.

'Nikos,' she breathed, as his arms wrapped around her from behind and her spine warmed itself against his hair-roughened chest.

'Hush,' he said. 'Go to sleep.'

He soothed his hand over her rough thigh and for a moment

she went rigid in his arms, and then, with a little sigh, she relaxed again.

Slowly, soothingly, he smoothed the scarred and runnelled skin, as if it were lustrous marble.

CHAPTER TEN

HIS hand was still covering her thigh when she awoke. Sunlight pressed against the heavy drapes, dimly illuminating the oppressively decorated bedroom. She felt the bed swaying slightly, she thought, and remembered that this was no ground-based dwelling, but that they were afloat upon the bosom of the sea.

When she stirred, Nikos did too. And as he moved she realised, with a little gasp, that as she lay spoon-like, back against him, his body was taking notice of the fact.

He felt it too, the moment he surfaced into consciousness. The same sense of ruefulness he had felt last night filled him. Whatever his leap of appetite right now, he must not risk hurting her.

Besides, he thought encouragingly, abstinence now would bring its own rewards later.

So he stretched backwards and away from her, languorously extending his limbs before lithely jack-knifing and getting out of bed.

'This morning,' he announced, 'we shall have breakfast in bed. And then more sightseeing!'

He certainly needed something, Nikos thought, throwing on his bathrobe before striding to the phone to order breakfast, to divert him from what he really wanted to do right now.

Sightseeing would do as well as anything.

In fact, he acknowledged later, it had its own compensations. It was another glorious day, fresh and sweet in the early summer. Setting off in the four-by-four, Nikos at the wheel, they merged into the general throng of holidaymakers.

They headed for Samaria and the famous gorge. Andrea had

154

read about it in the guidebook Nikos had bought for her before they left Rethimnon.

'I know I can't walk it,' she said, 'but at least I can see it.'

Nikos took her as close as he could, driving deep into the heart of the White Mountains of western Crete. They drank coffee on the terrace of the little *cafeneion* near the start of the walk, the Xiloskala, wooden stairs that led into the gorge. Above them towered the bare, bleak heights of the Gingalos peak, skirted by rock and scree.

'Tomorrow we'll sail round to the mouth of the gorge, Agia Roumeli, and cruise along the southern coast,' said Nikos. 'In fact—' he glanced at his watch '—we have time to drive down to Sougia today, if you wish.'

Andrea nodded, happy to go anywhere with him. 'What does *agia* mean?' she asked. 'There are so many places called "Agia" something or other.'

Nikos laughed. 'Saint—a female saint. Male saints are *agios*.' He looked at her a moment. 'You must learn the language of your forefathers, Andrea *mou*. Now that you are to live here.'

She was silent. Emotions racketed around inside her. Nikos was opening doors she must keep shut.

'What about *mou*?' she asked. She did not want to think about what he had said. 'You keep saying, "Andrea *mou*".'

'*Mine,*' he said softly. The grey eyes held hers. 'My Andrea.'

She looked away, her face troubled.

She felt the brush of his fingers on her hand.

'I have made you mine, have I not, Andrea *mou*?' he murmured.

Colour stole into her cheeks, feeding the tumult in her heart.

I can't think about this! I can't think about anything!

She swallowed. 'Where are we heading next?' she said brightly. 'I'm starting to get hungry!'

His fingers closed around hers, his thumb lazily smoothing her skin. 'So am I, *agape mou*, so am I...'

But it was a hunger he was to be prevented from sating for many hours to come. Even so, he consented to be her holiday companion, her fellow-explorer, willingly enough. She was a different person, it seemed to him, here on Crete. The reserved, composed, controlled Englishwoman who was such hard work to entertain, whom he had got used to squiring around Athens, had transformed into a vibrant, open personality who was a delight to be with. Was it just because the appalling tensions of the last weeks had finally resolved themselves? Or was it because he had made her his own?

For she was his own now; he knew that. No other man would ever touch her. She was his wife. Already he cherished her. A surge not just of possession but of protectiveness speared through him whenever he looked at her. No man would hurt her again, for she would need no other man now. Only him.

The future looked bright. Brighter than ever he had dared hope.

All that panic-generated talk she had spouted at him on their wedding night about leaving him in the morning was nothing. It had been her fears speaking; that was all. And those fears he had shown to be nothing more than phantasms haunting her.

He had exorcised her ghosts, he knew, and from now on their path was clear and thornless.

This rushed arranged marriage would work out for them— he was sure of that now. Together they would move on through the years ahead.

Well-being filled him, and the future was bright with promise.

At his side, as they zig-zagged down the winding road through the lovely Agia Irini gorge towards the southern coast, Andrea could not stop herself from looking at him.

Her breath caught every time she did so. It was everything about him—everything! From the satin sheen of his dark hair, the impossible glamour of his sunglasses, the firm, sensual line of his mouth, the vee of his open collar, the flexible strength of his hands curving around the wheel of the car, the tanned sinews of his bare forearms—all, all made her want to drink him in, feast her eyes on him more and more.

And yet while her senses feasted her emotions swirled within her. His words at the *cafeneion*, about learning Greek, had filled her with dismay.

How could she live here, in Greece? How could she be truly married to Nikos Vassilis?

It was unthinkable!

And yet, and yet…

Too much pulled at her. Too many emotions.

I can't think about it! I just can't!

She knew she would have to, eventually. Knew that the future was looming over her like a dark, overpowering wall. But for now she would turn her back on it.

She had a few days' grace, she knew. The quick staccato phone call she had made to Tony from the bedroom, before they had set off for Knossos yesterday, had simply communicated an unforeseen change of plan. He had been worried, she could tell, for all she had said was that she was fine, but would not be coming home quite yet; she would let him know when.

'I'm not at my grandfather's house,' she had reassured him rapidly. 'I'm…I'm…somewhere else…with someone else.'

Tony had been alarmed, despite her use of the code word they had agreed.

'Where else?' he demanded.

'I'm on my grandfather's yacht,' she had admitted. 'But he's not here. I'm OK, truly. I have to go; someone's coming! Give my love to Mum. I'll be home soon—promise.'

But would she be home soon? She stared out of the windscreen, out over the alien landscape of Crete.

What am I doing? What am I doing?

She had no answer. She was adrift on a new ocean, carried by an unstoppable tide.

At her side, Nikos slipped his left hand from the wheel and took her hand, sensing her troubled frame of mind.

'All will be well, Andrea *mou*. Trust me.'

For now there was nothing else for her to do.

For now it was enough.

*   *   *

They had lunch in the little town of Sougia, at a tourist taverna overlooking the shingle beach.

'It is a pity you are not up to walking,' remarked Nikos. 'There is, so I have just been told, a very popular walk to a place called Ancient Lissos—it is a Roman site, small, but very pretty. Perhaps we can land there from the yacht, another day. You cannot get there by road, I understand.'

'Is it a long walk?' Andrea asked.

'About an hour, the waiter told me, but it could be rough, and I don't want to risk it.'

'I'm sorry to be such a drag on you,' Andrea said quietly.

He took her hand. 'You are not a drag. You have done your best against great odds. I cannot begin to think what you must have gone through.'

His kindness nearly undid her. She felt tears misting her eyes. He saw them, and patted her hand encouragingly.

'No, do not cry, Andrea. As you said to me yourself, there are others so much worse off!' His gentling smile took any reproof from the words. 'And think too how much worse it would have been, what you went through, had you not been cushioned by your grandfather's wealth. I know that money cannot buy health, but it can buy comfort, and freedom from financial stress, in ways you cannot, perhaps, imagine. Your mother could afford the best treatment for you, the best doctors, the best care—it is something to be grateful for, *ne*?'

Cold drenched through Andrea. Cushioned by her grandfather's wealth? She saw again, vivid in her mind, the letter from his office, replying, finally, to the desperate pleadings of her mother after Kim had sent Yiorgos Coustakis all the medical reports on his granddaughter, detailing all the injuries she had suffered, recommending operations and physiotherapy that were so extensive, so expensive, that only private health care could provide for the years it would take to complete the treatment. The reports had been returned, accompanied by a terse letter to the effect that they were obviously gross exaggerations, and it was clearly nothing more than a ploy by a mercenary gold-digger to extort money from a man she had no claim on whatsoever.

And then Andrea chilled even more at the recollection of the final letter that had come, not from her grandfather, but from his lawyers, informing Kim that any further attempt at communicating with Yiorgos Coustakis would result in legal action.

Nikos watched her face shadowing. He had not meant to be harsh, but it was true, what he had said. Like so many born to wealth, Andrea seemed to take it all for granted. Oh, she was polite to servants, waiters and so on, but she never seemed to appreciate just how privileged her upbringing had been. In fact, he mused, she seemed to take more pleasure in something like a simple meal at a cheap taverna than in the lavish delicacies of a five-star restaurant...

If she'd had to work for her money, as he had done, she might appreciate the finer things of life more, he thought.

And do you appreciate anything else any more? Or will only the finest do for you now?

The quizzing voice sounded unwelcome in his mind, and he put it aside. He deserved his wealth—he had worked day and night to get where he was now. And Coustakis Industries was his rightful prize.

And the Coustakis heiress....

His mood lightened, and he lifted her imprisoned hand to his lips, grazing it lightly.

'I long for tonight, my sweet, passionate Andrea. I long for it—and you.'

Colour stained her cheekbones as she read the message in his eyes, and he sat back, well pleased.

Right now life was good. Very good.

And the night was even better. All the rest of the day Andrea found her awareness of Nikos mounting and mounting—during the drive back to the north of the island, during dinner eaten by the harbour in Chania, this time, not Rethimnon, and the drive back across the isthmus of the Akritori peninsula to the deep water of Souda Bay, where the yacht was moored. That night she hardly noticed the garish décor of the staterooms, hardly noticed the polite greetings of the crew, only noticed the way Nikos's eyes looked at her, wanting her, wanting her.

Desire swept through her, and the moment they gained the privacy of their bedroom she turned to him, and he to her. That night their coming together was even more incendiary—she knew now, so well, just what passion and desire, unleashed, could bring, and she revelled in it.

She felt wild and wanton, desirable and daring.

'I do believe,' Nikos murmured to her, his eyes glinting wickedly as she climbed astride him at his urging, eager to find more and more ways of showing her desire for him and sating her own, 'that you are making up for lost time.'

He slid his hands helpfully under her smooth, round bottom, lifting her up and positioning her exactly where he wanted her to be. Then he relaxed back.

'Take me.' The eyes glinted even more wickedly, making her feel weak with desire. 'I'm yours…'

She looked down at him, her red hair streaming like a banner down her naked back.

And slowly, tasting every moment of the experience, she came down on him. Possessing him.

It was the first of numberless possessions, each giving and taking as much as the other, their appetites feeding on each other, inflaming each other, sating each other, long into the following day. They did not go ashore that morning, letting Captain Petrachos take the yacht westwards, to round the island into the Libyan Sea and nose along the southern coast. Though the day was warm, and fine, Andrea and Nikos found a strange reluctance to take the fresh air.

'We should get up,' murmured Andrea, nestled against Nikos's hard-muscled chest.

'It's our honeymoon, Andrea *mou*. There is no hurry. We have all the time in the world.' He began to nuzzle at her tender earlobe, and she felt—extraordinary though it was, considering how short a time ago they had come together this latest time— her body beginning to respond to his caressing. 'On the other hand,' he considered, 'perhaps we should get up. Of course...' his teeth nipped gently, arousingly at her lobe '...we would need to have a bath first...'

Making love in a Jacuzzi was, Andrea discovered, a breathtaking experience, and one that lasted a long, long time. It was after noon before they finally emerged on to the deck, to take a long, leisurely lunch under an awning as the mountainous coastline of southern Crete slipped slowly past them. After lunch the launch was lowered, and Nikos took her first, as he had promised, to the tiny cove of Ancient Lissos, to explore the remains of the *asklepieion*—healing centre—and then sailing onwards, past the pretty whitewashed village of Loutro, along the piratical Sfakiot coastline until they made landfall at a beach marked on the map as 'Sweetwater Beach'.

'What a strange name,' said Andrea, and marvelled when she was shown the reason. Tiny freshwater springs pearled from beneath the pebbles. Andrea scooped some of the water to her lips.

'It *is* fresh!' she exclaimed in wonder.

It was such a beautiful afternoon, and the beach—unreachable by road—so relatively uncrowded, that they stayed to enjoy it. As Andrea started to relax, Nikos produced a swimsuit from amongst the towels.

'No one will look at your legs, Andrea,' he told her. 'They will all be too busy looking at your glorious figure.' He leant and kissed her softly. 'You are so beautiful. Your legs do not matter. Not to me. You must know that by now—you must!' He smiled cajolingly. 'Do it for me, my beautiful bride.'

How can I refuse? she thought. How can I refuse him anything?

Handing her a vast towelling changing tent, he helped her slip on the plain black one-piece he had acquired for her. As she stepped free she felt overcome with self-consciousness, but after a while she realised it was true—the others on the beach, scattered as they were, were not looking at her.

'Come,' said Nikos. 'That sea looks too tempting!'

He was stripping off before she could reply, baring every-

thing down to a pair of trunks under his trousers, and then he
was taking her hand and leading her into the clear water.

This early in the year the water had a bite to it that made
her gasp, but Nikos only laughed. He drew her in relentlessly,
and then, letting go, dived into the turquoise water, surfacing
to shake a shower of diamonds from his head.

'Come on! You'll thank me!'

And she did. When they finally emerged, some fifteen
minutes later, she felt glorious, reborn. He swathed a towel
around her and sat her down, pausing only to run a towel over
his back before joining her.

He grinned at her. She grinned back. The water on his long
eyelashes caught the sun, his damp, towel-dried hair made her
ache to touch it, and the expression in his eyes as he looked
at her made her weak.

All that marred her pleasure was the prospect of having to
go back on board her grandfather's yacht. It oppressed her
more and more. Not just because of the tasteless extravagance
of its opulent décor, but because it reminded her, as she did
not want to be reminded, of just why she had come to Greece
at all.

And she did not want to think of that.

'Nikos?' She sat up, looking at him questioningly. 'Do we
have to stay on the yacht?'

'You don't want to?' He sounded surprised. He didn't know
a woman who wouldn't have adored to luxuriate on board such
a floating palace!

But then Andrea, he was beginning to realise, was like no
woman he had ever known...

For so many reasons.

She shook her head.

'Can't we stay here, on Crete?'

He smiled indulgently. 'Of course. I will phone the yacht
and book a suitable hotel. Or would you prefer a private villa?'

'Can't we just take our chances? Wander around, stay where
we want? There are rooms to let everywhere, and we've passed
many little hotels in the Jeep.'

He looked at her. 'You'd like that?'

'Oh, yes! They look such fun. I've never done anything like that—'

Her voice was full of longing. How ironic, thought Nikos, that for someone raised in luxury, the commonplace was exotic!

He smiled lazily at her. 'Your wish, my most lovely bride, is my command!'

For five, wonderful, unforgettable days Andrea toured the island with Nikos. For five searing, incandescent nights she flamed with passion in his arms. All cares were left behind. This was a special time, she thought—all she would have. She must make the most of it. Make the most of Nikos.

She knew, with a terrible clenching of her heart, that it would be all she would have of him. The realisation struck like a cold knife at her

She heard his words at Knossos echo in her heart—'*We must live while we can, Andrea. We have no other choice except to make the most of what is given to us. Our minds, our hearts— our bodies and our passions.*'

And she *would* make the most of it—draw every bead of happiness, every pulse of pleasure and desire, every moment of calm, quiet bliss.

And make it last her all her life.

But I want it to last for ever!

That was impossible, she knew. This time with Nikos was nothing more than a brief, magical sliver of time. It shimmered with radiance, but it could not last.

Reality had to return, and she must accept that. Not willingly, but with a heavy, heavy heart. She knew, more than any, just how brief a portion of happiness life could hold. Her mother was testament to that. And yet she knew, for she had asked her once, that her mother would never have forgone the brief, fleeting bliss she had had with the man she loved, however long the empty years since then.

And I will be the same…

As they drove into Souda on their last evening on Crete, the setting sun turning the sea to gold, and saw the yacht moored there, Andrea's spirits became heavy. Her happiness was coming to an end and would never come again.

She looked across at Nikos, etching every line of his face into her memory.

I love him, she thought. I love him.

As the words formed in her mind she knew them for a truth she could never deny. Never abandon.

And never tell.

Andrea paced the deck of the yacht as it headed steadily, remorselessly, north in the starlight towards Piraeus. To the east the sky was beginning to lighten. It must be near dawn, she thought. Inside, Nikos lay asleep, exhausted by passion.

Our last time together, she thought in anguish.

She had slipped noiselessly away, needing—oh, needing solitude to think. To agonise.

This wasn't supposed to happen! This was never in the plan! I never meant to fall in love with him!

She stared blindly out over the sea, feeling the deck swell with the waves beneath the hull. The hull of a luxury Greek yacht.

This wasn't real—none of it was real! It was nothing more than a dream, a chimera. Reality was at home, in that drab council flat where she had lived all her life, bowed down by the debts that hung around Kim's neck—the money she had borrowed at ruinous interest, unsecured as it had to be, since they owned nothing of value, to pay for the private treatment Andrea had needed to make her walk again.

That's what I came to Greece for—to free her from that burden at last. To set her free from the cage and let her have some happiness in life at last, some comfort and ease.

And there was nothing stopping her—the money her grandfather had paid her to marry Nikos Vassilis was in her bank account. All she had to do was go home and spend it.

Leaving Nikos behind.

You'll never see him again! Never make love with him! Never hold him in your arms!

A cold wind gusted over her, and she shivered in the fine silk negligee.

So what? So what if you've fallen in love with Nikos Vassilis? He doesn't love you. He married you to get your grandfather's company. And if he seduced you, took you to his bed, made you his wife in deed as well as name, well, that is what a Greek husband would do with his bride—even one with crippled legs! Oh, he's been kind to you! Released you from your fears and made a woman of you! But he doesn't love you—and he doesn't want your love.

That was not in his plan. Don't think it was.

She hugged the negligee to her, but it could not keep out the cold that was seeping into her heart.

And how thrilled do you think he'll be when he discovers, as he must, that you are no more the precious Coustakis heiress than the Queen of Sheba? That you're nothing but the spurned, unwanted, bastard granddaughter of Yiorgos Coustakis, who's used you because he's got no one else to use to make a final stab at his own posterity! Do you think a man as rich as Nikos Vassilis wants a wife from a council flat?

She didn't even have to answer.

Desolation washed through her. Cold and empty.

At breakfast, taken indoors this time, as they made their way through the busy shipping lanes approaching Piraeus, Nikos, too, was not in the best of moods. The week away from Athens had made him forgot the pressures that would await him on his return. Tonight, and for the foreseeable future, he would be burning the midnight oil with a vengeance, as the process of merging Vassilis Inc and Coustakis Industries got underway. Already, before breakfast, he had been on the phone to his secretary, his directors, setting wheels in motion. But for the first time in his life he had no appetite for work.

Only for Andrea...

He felt his body stir, and crushed it ruthlessly. It would be at least late tonight before he was free to enjoy his passionate bride again. His jaw tightened. He would have to explain to her that their time together would be at a premium now. At least until he had completed his takeover of her grandfather's company.

Did she realise that already? She was not looking happy, he thought, studying her across the table. In fact, she looked different altogether. She had lost the casual, easygoing look she had had for the last week. Now she looked stiff, and tense, picking at her food.

'I'm sorry we couldn't have stayed away longer,' he said. 'But doing an M&A takes a lot of work.'

Andrea looked at him. He was wearing a business suit again, and it made him look formal. Distant. The man she had spent the most blissful week of her life with had vanished. In his place was the man who had married her to get hold of Coustakis Industries. And for no other reason.

She must remember that.

'I'm sure it does,' she said impersonally.

Nikos's mouth tightened. She was ready enough to accept the lavish lifestyle her family wealth afforded—but balked at how it had been earned in the first place.

'A corporate merger is not a trivial thing to accomplish, Andrea…'

He paused suddenly. There was a bleakness in her eyes he could not account for.

No, she thought, a corporate merger was not a trivial thing at all—it was something you could marry a stranger for!

And then make love to her until she fell in love with you— hopelessly, helplessly!

But he hadn't asked her to fall in love with him, she thought. He had asked for nothing more than a passionate companion for a week—a pleasant, relaxing interlude before resuming his real life. Making money.

Well, I made money out of it too, she thought defiantly. And now I'm going home to spend it. It's what I came for, and it's what I'm going home with.

Falling for Nikos was an aberration, a mistake. I'll go home and forget all about him.

I have to!

A steward came into the room and walked up to Nikos, saying something to him in Greek. Nikos nodded curtly, and the man hurried off.

Nikos got to his feet. He looked so tall, Andrea thought. And so devastating. Just the way he'd looked the first time she'd set eyes on him. It seemed a lifetime ago, not just a few short weeks.

Weeks that had changed her life for ever.

'Excuse me—but I have to take a phone call.' He sounded remote. Preoccupied.

She nodded. There seemed to be an immovable lump in her throat suddenly.

'Of course.'

Later, she stood on deck beside him, watching the yacht slide into its moorings. Then, later still, she sat beside him in the chauffeured limo driving them back to Athens. There was a third passenger, a young man introduced as Nikos's PA, and the moment the doors were closed the PA extracted a sheaf of papers and documents. In a moment he and Nikos were deep in business talk. Andrea looked out of the window.

She felt bleak, and sick, cold all the way through.

I'm leaving him, she thought. *I'm leaving him right now...*

The car made its slow way into Athens's business quarter, and as it finally pulled up outside Vassilis Inc she felt even bleaker, and sicker.

Nikos turned to her briefly.

'Yannis will drive you to the apartment. You must make yourself at home. I am sorry not to be able to accompany you myself, but something has come up—hence Demetrios's reception committee. I am sorry, but I could not avoid it. I will escape from the office as quickly as I can and we will have the evening together. Until then—'

He bent forward to kiss her.

She could not bear it. She jerked her head sideways, conscious, if nothing else, of the PA's presence. Nikos's kiss landed on her cold cheek.

Can you feel your heart break? thought Andrea, as Nikos climbed out of the car after his PA. Because mine broke, I know, just then.

She shut her eyes, leaning back into the seat. The car moved off.

Tears misted over her eyes.

After a while, she realised she would have to give the driver new instructions. He seemed surprised when she asked him to drive her to the airport, but did it dutifully enough.

On the way there she wrote a note. Every word drew blood from her heart.

> Dear Nikos
>
> I am going back to England. We have both got what we wanted out of this marriage. You got Coustakis Industries. I got my money. Thank you for our time together in Crete—you were a wonderful first lover. I'm sure you'll make a huge success of running Coustakis Industries. Please ask your lawyers to sort out our divorce as soon as possible. Thank you.
>
> Andrea.

It was all she could manage. And it cost her more than she could bear to pay.

She left it with the chauffeur to deliver it to Nikos.

CHAPTER ELEVEN

'WHAT do you think, Mum? Down on the coast or further up in the hills? Where do you want to live?'

Andrea's voice was bright and relentlessly cheerful, just as it had been since she had arrived back two weeks ago, bursting with the wonderful, glorious news that her grandfather, so she had told her mother, had given them enough money to settle their debts and allow them to move to Spain.

But, for all her determined high spirits, Andrea could see her mother was worried about her. Oh, she had been bowled over by the fantastic news about the money, which had settled their debts with a single cheque, and she had commented on how well Andrea looked with her sun-bronzed skin and burnished hair, and how she was walking, it seemed, with much greater confidence and assurance, but even so Andrea could sense Kim's concern.

She didn't want her mother worrying. Not about anything— least of all her. So she chattered away brightly as she prepared their evening meal, talking about Spain and the imminent prospect of living there. She was desperate to move as soon as possible. Perhaps, in Spain, starting her new life, she could start to forget Nikos...

Nikos—

Pain clenched at her heart. No—she mustn't think, mustn't remember. It was gone, over, finished. She was starting a new life now—that was the only important thing to think about. That and making Kim happy. She mustn't, *mustn't* let Kim suspect anything...

She mustn't see your heart is broken...

She smiled determinedly at Kim.

'It's going to be all right, Mum. Everything's going to be just wonderful from now on! Just wonderful!'

Kim smiled and took her daughter's hand. 'You are the best daughter a mother could have—always know that, my darling girl,' she said softly, her eyes searching her daughter's face.

'I love you so much,' Andrea choked, realising it had been worth everything just to know that she could at last repay her mother for her years of devotion. What did a broken heart matter?

The sudden imperative knocking on the front door made them both start.

Kim immediately looked nervous, and Andrea pugnacious.

'Ignore it, Mum. They'll try somewhere else.'

Increasingly wild and aggressive kids often did the rounds at this time of day, the early evening, knocking on doors to see if they could cadge money from anyone inside.

Thank God we're getting out of here, thought Andrea feelingly.

They would be in Malaga in forty-eight hours—not for good, just for a fortnight's flat-hunting—and Andrea could hardly wait. Searching for an apartment would occupy her mind. Stop her thinking, remembering…aching…

The knocking came again, even more imperative.

'Right,' said Andrea, 'I've had enough of this.'

She marched out of the kitchen and to the front door, ready to confront them, but the dark outline showing behind the strengthened frosted glass panel revealed a tall, masculine frame.

The demanding knocking came again, and Andrea heard the futile buzz of the broken doorbell being sounded. Like so much else on the estate, it was still waiting for the council to mend it.

As she yanked the door open to find steel-grey eyes blazing down at her, her heart stopped.

Nikos Vassilis stepped inside, forcing her to stumble backwards on numb, frozen legs.

'Don't *ever*,' he said in a voice that made her spine chill, 'walk out on me again.'

Shock drenched through Andrea, wave after cold wave. But beneath the disbelieving horror another emotion had seared like flame through her.

'How—how...?' she floundered.

'How did I track you down? With great difficulty, I assure you!' His voice grated the words. He glanced around disparagingly at the shabby, narrow hallway, its smell of damp quite perceptible. 'And with such a bolt-hole as this I am not surprised it took the investigators so long to find you! What is this dump?' His mouth twisted disdainfully at the evident poverty of her surroundings.

'This *dump*,' said a quiet voice from the kitchen doorway, 'is my home, Mr—?'

Andrea whirled. Kim was standing there, her expression wary and questioning.

'Vassilis,' supplied Nikos curtly. 'Nikos Vassilis. I have come for Andrea.'

'I'm not going with you!' Andrea cried out. She couldn't believe what was happening—couldn't believe it was really Nikos standing there, his svelte, expensive presence shrieking money, looking as out of place in the hallway of a tower block council flat as if he were an alien from another planet.

'What's going on?' asked Kim anxiously, coming forward.

'Nothing! Nothing at all,' Andrea replied instantly. 'Mr Vassilis,' she gritted, 'has made a mistake! He's leaving right now! Without me!'

'Wrong.' Nikos's voice was deadly. His eyes narrowed. 'Get your things—and make sure your passport is among them!'

'I'm not going anywhere!'

'You are going,' he ground out, 'back to Athens! You were somewhat premature in your departure, I must point out. You might have got the money you wanted from your grandfather—your main interest, was it not—?' his voice was scathing '—but your precipitate departure has made him feel...cheated.

He wants you back in Athens to fulfil your…obligations. Otherwise,' he spelt out, 'he will not proceed with the merger!'

It was her turn for her face to harden.

'Oh, well, we mustn't get in the way of the precious merger, must we?' she flared. 'That was, after all, *your* main interest, was it not?' Deliberately she echoed his words, confronting him with the truth of why he had ever looked twice at her!

It did not hit its mark.

'There were other…interests…as I recall… Ones that I fully intend to resume when you return to Athens to fulfil your…obligations. *Ne?*' His voice trailed off, but his eyes washed over her. Weakness flooded through her—and memory—hot, humid memory.

He saw it in her eyes, and smiled. A blighting smile that had no humour in it. 'You see, I too, Andrea *mou*, feel cheated by your precipitate and so *unexpected* departure.'

She heard the anger in his voice—suppressed, restrained, but savage beneath the words. There was something more than anger in it too, she realised. Something raw, and painful.

Then he had snapped his gaze past her, the tight, controlled mask back on his face, and rested it where Kim was hovering, a puzzled, anxious look on her face.

'I need to speak to Andrea. Privately. If you would be so kind—?'

'I've got nothing to say to you!' Andrea flashed back at him.

Steel eyes, flecked with gold, rested on her. 'But I,' he said with a softness that raised the hairs at the nape of her neck, 'have a great deal to say to you, Andrea *mou*.'

She felt faint, hearing him say her name, that had once been an endearment, now edged with scorn. Behind her, Kim stepped forward and closed her hand protectively around Andrea's arm.

'Mr Vassilis, if my daughter does not wish to speak to you—'

The rest of her words were cut off by a rasp sounding in Nikos's throat. Shock etched across his face, and his eyes flashed back to Andrea.

'This woman is your *mother*?' Disbelief was in every word.

It was Kim who answered. 'Yes, I am Andrea's mother, Mr Vassilis. And perhaps...' she took a faltering breath '...you would explain what is going on?'

Nikos's eyes were scanning from face to face, his eyes narrowed, comparing the two women. Andrea knew what he would see—she and Kim did not look much alike. Kim was slighter in build, and her hair was fair, greying now at the temples, her faded eyes blue. All that she had got from her mother was her bone structure and her fine skin. Her red hair had come from Kim's grandmother, she knew, and her chestnut eyes were a legacy from her father.

But whatever he saw must have convinced him. 'Mrs Coustakis—' he began. His voice sounded shaken, but determined none the less.

Kim shook her head. 'I'm Kim Fraser, Mr Vassilis. Andreas and I never married.'

Her words were quietly spoken, and not ashamed. She had, her daughter knew, nothing—*nothing*—to be ashamed of.

Shock etched across Nikos's face again. It stabbed at Andrea. Telling her everything she needed to know. Bitter, bitter though that knowledge was.

'You see—' she twisted the words out of her mouth '—I'm not the woman you thought I was! Look around you!' Her arm swept the narrow hallway. 'Do I look like an heiress? Living here?'

Her words were a bitter, defiant challenge.

'This isn't possible.' Nikos's voice was flat. His denial total.

She gave a mocking, angry laugh. She had known, always known, that he would be horrified to discover her humble origins—to discover she did not come from his rich, sophisticated world. After all, what would a man as rich as Nikos Vassilis want with a wife from a council flat?

He moved suddenly, a hand flattening on the door beside him that led into the living room, pushing it open. He walked in. The room was clean and tidy, but the carpet was cheap and worn, the chairs and sofa-bed where Andrea slept shabby and frayed.

'You live here?'

His voice was still flat. Andrea followed him in.

'Yes. All my life.'

'*Why?*'

The word exploded from him. Andrea gave a high, short laugh.

'Why? Because it's all Mum could afford, that's why! She lived on benefits until I was old enough to start school, and the council housed us here—she was lucky to get it, a flat of her own, a single, teenaged mother as she was! When I started school she got a part-time job, but it's hard work to put aside enough money to try and buy a place of your own when you've a child to bring up single-handed.'

'Single-handed? When your grandfather is Yiorgos Coustakis?' His voice was a sneer.

Her eyes flashed. 'Yiorgos Coustakis—' she ground out her grandfather's name with contempt '—told my mother she had no claim on my father's estate. She's brought me up on her own—totally.'

As she spoke, his lips compressed. He scanned the room again, taking in every last detail. His gaze hardened.

'Are you telling me,' he demanded, and his face was set, tight as a bow, 'that your grandfather does not support you?'

'That's right,' she said evenly. 'I told you—I'm not a Coustakis at all.'

Kim's voice intervened, sounding confused and distressed.

'Andrea, what about the money? You told me Yiorgos had given you all that money of his own free will! If you extorted it from in any way then you must give it back! You *must!*'

'No!' she cried, appalled. 'No! The money's yours, it's *yours* totally—to buy you an apartment in Spain, to pay your debts, to—'

'Debts?' Nikos pounced on the word. His face was still carved from stone.

'Yes,' said Kim, turning to him. 'I'm afraid, Mr Vassilis, I owe rather a lot of money. You see, when she was younger, Andrea had a very bad road accident. The therapy needed to enable her to walk again was only available privately, so I had to borrow money to pay for it. We're still paying it back— Andrea helps all she can. She has two jobs, and every penny she can spare goes towards it!'

Nikos looked numb, then he recovered.

'You never asked Yiorgos Coustakis to help you?' The question grated from him.

A harsh laugh escaped Andrea. 'Oh, Mum asked, all right! She went down on her knees to ask him to help her! She sent him all the doctors' reports on me—every last one of them! She begged him to help for the sake of his son—she promised she would repay the money as soon as she could.'

'And?' Nikos's voice was chill.

'He refused. He said she was trying to get money out of him by false pretences! His lawyers wrote telling Mum that if she tried to contact him again for any reason they'd take legal action against her for harassment.' She took a steadying breath, and went on. 'That's why I won't give the money back to him! Whatever Mum says! I've cleared her debts and I'm going to buy her a flat in Spain. There'll be enough change from the five hundred thousand pounds to invest safely for her and give her an income to live on, and a pension, and all that stuff, and—'

Nikos's face had stilled again. 'Five hundred thousand pounds?' His voice was hollow. 'Are you telling me that's what Yiorgos Coustakis paid out to you?'

She lifted her chin defiantly. 'I know it's a huge amount, but it's what I needed to get Mum sorted and settled.'

'Five hundred thousand,' he echoed. 'Half a million pounds.' His eyes blazed again suddenly. 'Do you have any *idea* how much your grandfather is worth?' He took a step forward and his hands closed around her forearms. He was close, much too close to her. 'Half a million is a pittance to him! A *pittance*!'

She jerked away.

'I don't care what he's worth! I don't care anything about

him! He treated Mum like dirt and I loathe him for it! I don't want more of his filthy money—I just wanted enough to get Mum out of here to somewhere safe and warm, with enough to live on without worrying the whole time! She's got asthma, and the damp in the flat makes her really ill...'

Her voice trailed off. He was not listening. He was staring around him, taking in every shabby detail.

That's right, thought Andrea viciously, pain stabbing at her as he looked round so disdainfully at the place she lived in. *Take a good look! This is where I come from! This is my home! Now you will despise me for it!*

Now, into the silence, Kim spoke.

'Mr Vassilis, I can see this has been an unwelcome shock to you, and I am sorry for that. But...' She hesitated, then went on. 'I would be grateful if you would please explain what the purpose of your being here is—'

His eyes flicked to her. 'My purpose? My purpose, Ms...Fraser—' he said her maiden name as if it pained him '—has just changed.'

Andrea's throat tightened. *I'll just bet it's changed! You came here to take me home with you and now you probably can't wait to get out of here as fast as you can...*

His attention suddenly swivelled to her. Her breath caught. His eyes were like slate, his face closed and shuttered.

And yet it was the face of the man she loved. Loved so much, so unbearably much!

I never thought I'd see him again! Thought I'd live the rest of my life without him! But he's here, now—

A vice crushed her heart.

Yes, and he's just about to walk out—for ever now he knows the truth about you.

A shaft of self-accusation hit her.

I should have been honest—right from the start. I deceived him—no wonder he is angry!

She took a deep, shuddering breath.

'Look, Nikos—I'm sorry. Truly. I didn't realise that my coming home would jeopardise your merger!'

A grim expression crossed his face. 'There is no merger. Nor will there be.'

No—how could there be? thought Andrea bleakly. Nikos Vassilis had thought he was marrying the Coustakis heiress— not the unacknowledged bastard of a woman Yiorgos Coustakis thought a gold-digging slut! Nikos had thought he was getting a wife who came from his world—not a girl who'd been born and bred in a decaying council flat.

'I should have told you,' she said heavily.

His eyes rested on her like unbearable weights. 'Yes, you should have told me, Andrea. You *should* have told me.'

'I'm sorry,' she said again. It seemed the only thing she could say.

'Are you?' There was something very strange in his voice. 'So am I.'

Well, of course he was. Andrea knew. Of course he wished he'd known from the start just how *tainted* she was! As if it wasn't bad enough to discover she was crippled—she was common as well...

Nikos's eyes had slid past her, lingering briefly on the tense, anxious figure of her mother, and then out, out through the window.

He wants to get out of here, Andrea thought. Get back to his own world. Where she had no place. Nor ever could have.

Through the window Nikos saw the other tower blocks of the estate and, far below, the world beneath. The sun was setting, starting to turn everything to gold. He stared down. All the kingdoms of the world spread before him.

He thought of the journey he had made—the long, hard journey from the streets of Athens—with only one focus, only one goal. Making money. More and more of it. Acquiring Coustakis Industries would have been the pinnacle of his achievement.

And he was a young man still. Who knew what kingdoms he could buy and sell before his time was up? Who knew what souls he could buy and sell with all his riches?

A face stole into his mind's eye. An old man's face, whose eyes knew well the price of a man's soul.

What is mine worth? thought Nikos. And the answer came clear. Clarion-clear.

Too much for Yiorgos Coustakis to pay.

He stepped away from the window and looked back at the two women in the shabby room. The kingdoms of the earth disappeared from view.

His hand slipped inside his jacket, taking out his mobile. He punched in a number. His voice, when he spoke, was curt. 'This is Nikos Vassilis. I have a message for Yiorgos Coustakis. Tell him I am standing in front of Kim Fraser and her daughter in their home—the merger is off.'

Then he disconnected.

As he slipped the phone back in his pocket his eyes met Andrea's.

She reeled.

The blaze of emotion in them was like a flash-flame.

'I will make him pay,' he said softly. 'If it takes me the rest of my life I will make him pay for what he has done to you.'

Andrea stared. His mouth twisted at her expression and he forged on. 'I knew the man was ruthless—all the world knew that! But that he would stoop so low... *Christos*, he has behaved like an animal!'

She couldn't speak—couldn't do anything but stare at him, disbelieving.

Nikos's eyes raced around the room again. 'To make you live like *this*,' he grated. 'To turn his back on his own flesh and blood—to leave you to struggle on your own all these years. Not even—' His voice hardened like the edge of a knife. 'Not even to lift a finger when his own granddaughter faced a lifetime in a wheelchair...' He shut his eyes. 'Dear God in heaven, what kind of scum is he?'

His eyes snapped open. They glinted like steel. He reached for his phone again. 'Well,' he said grimly, 'the world will soon know.'

Before Andrea's very eyes she saw him speak in English

again. 'Demetrios? Prepare a press-release. The Coustakis merger is off. Yes, you heard me. And I shall be making my reasons for pulling out very, very clear. The stink will reach heaven, I assure you! I'll phone again in an hour, when you've had time to contact the board.'

He snapped the phone off again.

'Mr Vassilis.' Kim spoke, her voice agitated and perturbed. 'Please—I don't understand any of this! What is happening?'

'What is happening...' Nikos's voice softened as he saw how disturbed Kim was '...is that I have decided not to take over Coustakis Industries. I refuse, absolutely—' his voice hardened again '—to have anything to do with a man who could behave in such a way to you and your daughter! I refuse, absolutely,' he finished, 'to do business of any kind with him!'

'But—but...' stammered Andrea. 'But the merger means so *much* to you—'

A hand slashed through the air. 'No. Only one thing means anything to me, Andrea.' His voice changed. 'Only one thing.'

He took a step towards her. She wanted to step back, but she couldn't. She was rooted to the spot.

'Don't you know what it is, Andrea *mou*?' His voice had softened. 'Surely you must know?' His hand reached out to touch the flaming aureole of her hair. Her breath caught. 'Surely?'

He looked down at her, his eyes flecked with gold. 'When you left me it was as if you had stabbed me to the quick. To the heart. I bled, Andrea *mou*. I bled.'

His fingers brushed her cheek, and she felt faint. 'Come back to me, *pethi mou*, come back to me—'

Her throat was tight, but she tore the words out. 'What for? If there's to be no merger then you don't have the slightest need of me!'

He smiled. Her heart turned over.

'Need? Oh, my Andrea, I need you to breathe. Without you I cannot live. Do you not know that?'

His hand cupped her cheek. 'I need you to light my way, to walk at my side all my life. I need you to be with me, every day and night.' His other hand closed around her other cheek, cupping her face, lifting it to his.

It was odd, Andrea thought. His face had gone out of focus; the flecks of gold in his eyes were misting. Something must be in her eyes—some mote of dust.

'But—' she swallowed '—but I don't see why you need me...'

He smiled, and it filled a gaping hole in her heart.

'Didn't I show you every night, every day we spent together? Didn't you show me?'

'Show you what?' she breathed. Her eyes were brimming now; she could not stop it.

He lowered his head and kissed her softly.

'That we were falling in love, Andrea *mou*.'

'Love?' It was a whisper, a breath.

'Oh, yes. Love—quite definitely love.' There was no doubt in his voice. None at all. 'There can be no other word for it. How else could the wound you dealt me when you left me have been so mortal to me? How else—' a finger lifted to her lashes and let the tears beading there spill onto him '—could these tears be making diamonds of your eyes?'

'But you don't love me—you can't—you don't have to! It was only because of the merger that you married me—'

The gasp from Kim went unheard.

'Our marriage, my sweet, most beloved Andrea, is the only good thing to come of that cursed merger! I always meant to make you a good husband, even when I thought ours was to be nothing more than a mutually beneficial arranged marriage. Once I would have been content with that. But on Crete—ah, then it became much, much more! And when I discovered you had left me, oh, I realised just how much more! The pain of losing you was agony—and I knew then that something had happened to me that I did not ever dream of. I had fallen in love with you—fathoms deep.' He looked down at her tenderly, possessively—lovingly.

'You can't love me...' Her voice was a whisper, a thread. 'We come from such different worlds. Look—'

She gestured helplessly with her hand at the shabby apartment.

He followed her gesture with his eyes, knowing now why she had said the same words to him on the night of their wedding. To think he had thought it was because she had been born to a wealth he'd had to fight all his life to acquire!

'When you return to Athens with me,' he said in a low voice—and there was a strangeness in it Andrea had never heard, 'I will show you were I was born—where I lived until I crawled from the gutter as a young man. A man, Andrea, who never knew his father, whose mother did not care whether he lived or died. A man, Andrea, who vowed—*vowed* he would make something of his life! I was determined to achieve the success and recognition I craved!'

He took a deep, shuddering breath, and Andrea stared at him, wordless, as suddenly—totally—she saw the man Nikos really was—not the gilded scion of a wealthy patrimony, but someone with the guts, the determination, the courage, to make something of himself out of the nothing he had been born with.

'But I have learnt...' his voice had softened, taken on a sense of wonder '...that true riches are not in gold and silver. True riches...' his eyes melted her, and she felt her heart turn over '...are here—inside us. I envy you so much, Andrea.' His eyes glanced across to where Kim stood staring, bemused and wondering. 'To have had the love of your mother—and I envy even more—' his voice, she thought, almost cracked '—your love for her. And so I ask you—beg you—' as he spoke her throat tightened to an unbearable tightness '—to accept my love for you—and to give me yours.'

He paused, looking down at her, gathering her hands against his heart.

'Come back to me, Andrea, and be the wife of my heart, for I love you more than I can bear.'

The tears were spilling down her cheeks now.

'Yes!' she uttered as he kissed her tears away, and then his mouth closed over hers, and what was the gentle, soft touch of homage became a salutation to the future they would have together.

He released her, and turned to face Kim. Andrea could see the tears shining in her mother's eyes.

'Have we your blessing?' Nikos asked her quietly.

For a moment her mother could not speak. And then, with a broken cry, she answered.

'Oh, yes! Oh, *yes*!'

EPILOGUE

'IF IT is a boy, then Andreas. If a girl, then Kim.'

Andrea smiled. 'Kim isn't very Greek.'

Her husband brushed this unimportant objection inside. His hand moved over the rounded contour of her belly.

'He kicked!' Nikos's voice was full of wonder—and astonishment.

'Or she,' pointed out Andrea. Her hand closed over Nikos's. She leant her head back against his shoulder, her gaze stretching out over the azure Aegean that spread all around them, feeling the familiar swell of the sea beneath the hull. 'How can I be so happy?' she asked.

With his free hand Nikos stroked her hair.

'Because you deserve it,' he said.

Andrea reached up to kiss him. 'And you do too.'

It seemed to her still such a miracle—to be so happy together. Since that magical, miraculous evening, when Nikos had come to claim her heart for his own, her life had turned upside down all over again. And she rejoiced in it totally!

Nikos had whisked them both off to Greece, sweeping Kim with them as well, and settled them in a hired villa on a private island.

'I don't want you exposed to what will happen now,' he had told Andrea. 'It will be very ugly.'

Then he had gone to Athens, to face Yiorgos Coustakis. His denouncement had been merciless—and so had the press coverage that had ensued. The scandal of the way one of the richest men in Greece had behaved to his own granddaughter had shocked the nation. That, and the cancellation of the expected merger with Vassilis Inc, had caused a steep plunge in the Coustakis share price, had precipitated the normally cowed

183

board of Coustakis Industries into drastic action. Yiorgos had been deposed as chairman, forced to retire, a social pariah.

The seizure that had killed him a month later had moved few to pity a man who had had no pity in him for anyone else, no kindness in his hard, selfish heart.

His entire fortune had passed to his despised granddaughter, for in his rage at his new son-in-law he had destroyed the will that had left his wealth to his future great-grandson, and Andrea had become, by default, the Coustakis heiress after all.

It was a troubling inheritance.

'Nikos—are you sure, very sure, about what you want me to do?' Her voice was anxious as she stood in the circle of his arms, looking out over the shining Aegean sea.

He turned her round to face him.

'Completely sure.' His answer came unhesitatingly. 'The Andreas Coustakis Foundation will be a fine and fitting monument to your father—and your mother is in agreement as well. After all,' he went on, 'all three of us know what it is to be poor, Andrea *mou*. The foundation will give a chance to so many children blighted by their families' poverty.'

Her eyes were still troubled. 'But we could keep the Coustakis shares, and you could run the company as you always intended…'

He shook his head decisively. 'No. We have more than enough money, Andrea—we will never be poor. To me, Yiorgos's wealth is tainted. His neglect of you proves it. Let it be put to good use now.' His mouth twisted. 'Perhaps if we use his wealth to some good end, people might have something pleasant to remember him by.'

'He was so vile to Mum, so needlessly cruel and offensive, and yet…' her voice sounded strained '…it was a miserable end for him—collapsing and dying alone, with not a soul to care about him.'

'But then, he did not care for anyone except himself,' Nikos answered soberly. 'You and your mother were not the only ones he injured—there were many victims of Yiorgos Coustakis. When the newspapers ran the story of his shameful treatment of you and your mother other stories came out too, showing his brutality, his ruthlessness, his absolute disregard for anyone else.'

He took her hand. 'And now the Coustakis fortune is yours. Let it do some good for others, for a change—as Yiorgos Coustakis never did. Come,' he said, starting to stroll down the deck with her, 'we might as well make the most of our farewell cruise on this floating monument to execrable interior yacht design!'

Andrea laughed. 'I'm sure some billionaire somewhere will love it—and that hideously gilded house he lived in as well! The sale of both will boost the coffers of the foundation handsomely!'

'Indeed. However,' Nikos mused, 'I think perhaps we ought to see if we can persuade Captain Petrachos not to leave us—I'm sure we can find some way of tempting him to stay. He was saying over dinner last night that he would be happy to help with the seamanship aspects of the youth training programme for the foundation.'

Andrea exchanged glances with him. 'Funnily enough,' she commented dryly, 'that was the very thing Mum said she was keenest on helping to set up. A striking coincidence, wouldn't you say?' Her voice changed. 'Oh, I do so hope that something might come of them being together! I always dreamed of Mum meeting someone else—I know she was so in love with my father, but if she could find companionship, at least, it would be so wonderful for her!'

Nikos smiled. 'Let us wish them well—for we have happiness and enough to spare, *ne*, Andrea *mou*?'

She wound her arm around him.

'I do love you, Nikos,' she said, 'so very much.'

He stopped, and turned her in his arms, and kissed her.

'And I love you, Andrea *mou*. Through all the years we have.'

The future, as bright and golden as the sun pouring over the Aegean sea, beckoned to them, and they walked towards it together.

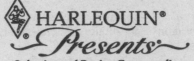
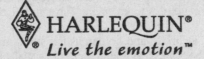

The world's bestselling romance series.

HARLEQUIN®
Presents

Seduction and Passion Guaranteed!

We are pleased to announce
Sandra Marton's fantastic new series

The **O'CONNELLS**

In order to marry, they've got to gamble on love!

Don't miss...

KEIR O'CONNELL'S MISTRESS

Keir O'Connell knew it was time to leave Las Vegas when he became
consumed with desire for a dancer. The heat of the desert must have
addled his brain! He headed east and set himself up in business—
but thoughts of the dancing girl wouldn't leave his head.
And then one day there she was, Cassie...

Harlequin Presents #2309
On sale March 2003

**Pick up a Harlequin Presents® novel and you will enter a world
of spine-tingling passion and provocative, tantalizing romance!**

Available wherever Harlequin books are sold.

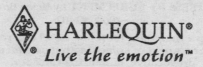

HARLEQUIN®
Live the emotion™

Visit us at www.eHarlequin.com

HPTOCON

The world's bestselling romance series.

HARLEQUIN®
Presents

Seduction and Passion Guaranteed!

It used to be just a nine-to-five job...
until she realized she was

In Love With Her Boss

Now it's an after-hours affair!

In Love With Her Boss

**Getting to know him in the boardroom...
and the bedroom!**

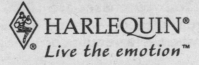

If you enjoyed what you just read,
then we've got an offer you can't resist!

Take 2 bestselling love stories FREE!

Plus get a FREE surprise gift!

Clip this page and mail it to Harlequin Reader Service®

IN U.S.A.	**IN CANADA**
3010 Walden Ave.	P.O. Box 609
P.O. Box 1867	Fort Erie, Ontario
Buffalo, N.Y. 14240-1867	L2A 5X3

YES! Please send me 2 free Harlequin Presents® novels and my free surprise gift. After receiving them, if I don't wish to receive anymore, I can return the shipping statement marked cancel. If I don't cancel, I will receive 6 brand new novels every month, before they're available in stores! In the U.S.A., bill me at the bargain price of $3.57 plus 25¢ shipping & handling per book and applicable sales tax, if any*. In Canada, bill me at the bargain price of $4.24 plus 25¢ shipping & handling per book and applicable taxes**. That's the complete price and a savings of at least 10% off the cover prices—what a great deal! I understand that accepting the 2 free books and gift places me under no obligation ever to buy any books. I can always return a shipment and cancel at any time. Even if I never buy another book from Harlequin, the 2 free books and gift are mine to keep forever.

106 HDN DNTZ
306 HDN DNT2

Name	(PLEASE PRINT)	
Address	Apt.#	
City	State/Prov.	Zip/Postal Code

* Terms and prices subject to change without notice. Sales tax applicable in N.Y.
** Canadian residents will be charged applicable provincial taxes and GST.
  All orders subject to approval. Offer limited to one per household and not valid to current Harlequin Presents® subscribers.
® are registered trademarks of Harlequin Enterprises Limited.

PRES02   ©2001 Harlequin Enterprises Limited

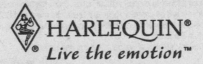